I0723973

CAPTAIN RANDOM AND THE RAINBOW CHASERS

HAYDEN GRIBBLE

ISBN 978-1-9998659-6-2

Printed and bound by Lightning Source, Milton Keynes

www.haydengribbleauthor.com

For William

Also by the author

The CAPTAIN RANDOM Adventures

Captain Random vs the Sandman
Captain Random and the Eater of Souls

Other titles by the author

The Man In The Corner
Tales From Another Me
Child Out Of Time: Growing Up With Doctor Who In
The Wilderness Years
The Lurking

I

All that Lon ever wanted was to be remembered.
To achieve all he could in life.

Nothing was unobtainable, if he really wanted it.

Notoriety and success went hand-in-hand in his
business and he liked it that way.

As the catacombs of Druis spiraled further and
further into the darkness, he licked his lips as his
latest prize drew him nearer.

He hadn't been the brightest at school, and yet he
aced every examination he was subjected to by the
harsh, totalitarian lecturers at Moftola University.
He wasn't the quickest on the track either, not by a
long shot, but he took part in arduous marathons
and, through sheer persistence and drive, he
always found a way to finish first.

His mansion on the sunny side of Milas XII, a
pleasure asteroid that circled a dwarf star in one of
the most exclusive and desired settlements in the
outer cosmos, renowned for its beautiful views of
the cosmic ballet between the nebulas and the stars.
Also, it was tax free and renowned for that too.

A nobody would never afford such a luxurious
place to call his home.

Lon was far from a nobody.

He was acclaimed prolific in his field of
intergalactic archaeology.

It had been his chosen subject back on his home planet. Maftola had a reputation in the Senas quadrant for breeding explorers and Lon was determined to be the best of the bunch.

Alfred Wolenhein, the man who found the lost treasure of Algonia? Lon wanted to make him a mere footnote in his planet's history.

Catalonia Trenaman, the first woman to uncover the hidden secrets of Rinan Berksop's latter day etchings on the inner mountains of Lagonias Valor? He wanted to leapfrog her achievements.

There was Tred Walterquintan too, the quantum-time award-winning emotion wanderer who posed as a hippy on the planet Earth and found the secret recordings of Jimi Hendrix. The songs were so magnificent that if any being played them, they'd be so good that they could render the listener unable to listen to anything else ever again. They were stored in a container that became so hot they liquidated, finally decomposing into a gas compound that escaped Tred's home . They were eventually found drifting in space in a state of detune, their power tempered. Now they merely gave the listener a psychedelic trip so magnificent they had to sleep for nine days just to shake the bad vibes out of their system. Well…Lon was working on beating that guy too.

And if he found what he was close to now…he would.

The Zedron Flux.

A helix of pure energy, binding the forces of Druis together in a way that could sustain the planet for a dozen millennia, at least according to the estimation of experts.

If he found it, it could save the universe.

Fossil fuels would be a thing of the past. Worlds like the Earth would no longer have to resort to polluting its atmosphere with the filth and grime mined from within its bowels.

Even solar energy would be a thing of the past.

The Zedron Flux was the ultimate goal.

If Lon found it, the cosmos would be saved.

And he could retire a hero, a name never forgotten by the generations who would live in the safe knowledge that their species would go on, in perpetuity.

Money is a reward worth pursuing.

Immortality is all the sweeter.

Lon was now so close he could taste it on the tip of his tongue.

Legend had it that the Flux, a true holy grail in the legends of the universe, would also give unimaginable power to the person who obtained it, who could wield it towards their every desire.

The Flux had the power to make Lon, if he wanted, a god.

'Nearly there, boss.'

Etherton removed his glasses to mop his brow then returned them to his face.

'What makes you so sure?' said another voice.

Auger was irritated by her counterpart's spasms of optimism. 'You've been saying that every few minutes since we got in this place.'

'Well, forgive me, dear lady, if my enthusiasm is somewhat premature, but I firmly believe that the heart of the catacombs is right this way.'

'Would you two put a sock in it? We'll find it when we find it,' whispered Lon.

'Sorry, Lon,' said Etherton sheepishly.

He shot a look to Auger, who was doing her best to not be ticked off by either of her companions. It was common for Lon to get anxious on occasion, especially when he was honing in on a promise of a brilliant discovery.

But on this trip he had seemed a little…tense. Normally, Lon had a twinkle in his eye when he told them off for their usual bickering.

Auger frowned. She didn't see the usual smirk either.

The twinkle had been extinguished for the time being.

Lon wiped the sweat from his brow.

'Damn it,' he cursed, 'Is it me or is it starting to get really hot down here?'

Etherton nodded.

'It certainly feels like it.'

'That must mean that we are close!' cried Auger.

Her bespeckled counterpart removed his glasses once again and blinked hard.

'I thought eyebrows were supposed to stop sweat from going in your eyes?' he groaned. 'Mine must be broken.'

'Don't be silly, old man,' Auger reassured.

'Auger's right. Just a little further,' cried Lon.

They passed a pillar that bore an old cave drawing. Etherton resisted temptation to down tools for a moment and study the curious etchings. Out of the three, it was he who regularly spotted those little details, the out of the ordinary, things which acted as clues as to what they were looking for. But since the group leader was preoccupied with his aim and seemed to be a bit on the nervous side, he thought he'd mention it on their return trip out of the catacombs instead, which was a shame, because he'd never get a chance to go back. But if they had stopped and followed the markings, they'd have learnt a great deal about the Zedron Flux and how it came to the depths of the planet Druis in the first place.

In the ancient times, the galaxy was ruled by almighty beings, omnipotent gods.

After a couple of millennia, they got bored of the wonders of the cosmos and, surprisingly, thought themselves out of existence.

There was nothing else to do now that the beings that made up the population of their creation were running amok, entirely untamable.

But before they did, they stored elements of their power in strategic places across the stars. All of them had perished over time, it was thought, except this one. The Flux was the glue that kept the energy of the universe bound together, and if it were to be harnessed correctly, it could save parts of the cosmos that needed its power most of all.

For Lon, and his two counterparts, it would mean galaxy-wide fame and adoration.

Not to mention wealth.

Ultimate power - at least, for one of them.

The light was pulsating a brilliant green, bright and alluring to the explorers, drawing them closer and closer. Finally, the team rounded the final wall and witnessed the magnificence of the Zedron Flux.

The Flux bore a resemblance to a double helix, a compound of molecules which forms the very DNA of all living things in the history of creation. Only this one was roughly two feet in height, almost a foot wide, and around it swarmed a glow of the most beautiful emerald either Lon, Auger or Etherton had ever seen.

Lon practically salivated at its sheer majesty. 'Behold, my friends, the element that keeps the entire cosmos alive, for centuries thought lost, a legend throughout the ages, before us now. Never forget this moment. We are the first people in all history to have gazed at its wonder. Etherton, make sure you're getting plenty of pictures.'

The small man just stood there, mouth gaping open, unable to take his eyes off the Flux.

'Etherton?' Auger tore herself away and nudged her counterpart.

He instantly reacted, fumbled within his satchel and dug out a rusted, yet modern looking device. He flipped a switch on the side and held it as it unfurled into the form of a rather old-fashioned camera.

'Won't the flash harm it?'

'Not at all, Etherton. The Flux is pure energy, remember? If it can provide the life force for all life forms who have ever lived, I'm sure it can withstand a flash from your camera bulb!'

'How do we take it, Lon?' asked Auger.

'Finally, a sensible question,' Lon searched inside his rucksack. He pulled out a long spherical tube and upon further rummaging, a set of thick gloves. 'When I was studying the awesome power of the Flux, I thought it would be best to come prepared.'

'Yes, but will the tube withstand its power?' said Etherton.

'Ah, ever the cynic, Etherton,' sneered Lon.

He turned to meet his friends in the eyes.

'There's only one way to find out.'

The intrepid explorer began to pull the gloves on.

'Good thing he brought those ones with him, all I could offer him are my gardening gloves!' muttered Etherton to Auger.

The team was standing a full ten feet away from the Flux but with extreme trepidation, Lon began to edge closer, taking one step at a time. He opened the tube, a hiss emitting from the void inside. As they neared the Flux, they were struck by the lack of sound coming from it.

'Lon, why is it so silent? I expected the Flux to be bristling with energy, didn't you?'

'Auger, please, not now. We'll discuss why's and how's later,' Lon spat. His pupils were green from the glow of the Flux as it span, levitating above the ground like a ballerina in midair.

Lon thought he could hear angels sing in his mind. This was it. This was the moment he became a legend. The moment he became a King.

With one final step he was awash with green light, almost at one with the Flux. He held his arms outstretched like a toddler walking towards its mother. He took a deep breath, ignoring the sweat cascading down his nose. Blinking back tears of joy, he lurched forward and held the Flux within his grasp.

Only he didn't.

He reached for the Flux again.

His fingers disappeared through the green light and failed to make contact with anything.

'What's going on?' asked Auger.

Lon tried desperately again and again and then another time but to no avail.

'The Flux…it's not here!'

'What are you talking about Lon?' said Etherton.

'It's a hologram!' he replied.

'It can't be! What's creating the heat then?'

'That would be me, I'm afraid.'

A fourth voice entered the fray. It sounded muffled, like it was coming through a communications device.

'I do hope you can hear me. We are quite far away from your current location.'

Lon's eyes narrowed with murderous intent.

'Strakonis! You'll pay for this!'

The voice at the other end of the device crackled with laughter.

'I doubt it. Even as we speak, we are light years away from Druis. You were just too late on this occasion. Still, can't win them all. Isn't that what you used to tell me?'

Lon's fists clenched tight.

'I refuse to be beaten by you.'

'That's the trouble with you, Lon. You never know when to give up. Fine, well, if you can find us, which I certainly doubt, we'll talk it over then. Hey, maybe I'll even let you hold the Flux, so you can have a little moment of glory at least? Until next time, my friend.'

The communicator fizzed out of life.

Etherton looked at Auger with a terrified look in his eye. He knew how much this meant to all of them, but to Lon?

This was supposed to be his crowning glory, his final job. And knowing his boss the way he did, he knew that Lon would not take this defeat well.

Lon never lost. Ever.

The explorer fell onto his haunches and howled.

'He is not getting away with this. I will not rest until Strakonis lies ruined, penniless in a hole in the ground!'

'Steady on, Lon,' Auger nervously interjected.

He got up and pushed his face right up to Auger's.

'Nobody tells me what to do. Not today, not any day. Do you understand!?'

She nodded hastily.

Slimeball, she thought to herself. It was about time you were knocked down a peg or two.

'Er, I hate to be the bearer of more bad news, but I think I've discovered the cause of the heating issue down here.'

Lon turned back to Etherton who was studying a split in the ceiling above where the hologram of the Flux had been cunningly placed by Strakonis. The heat was ebbing through the crack, which was widening second by second.

A tremor began to quake the explorers off balance.

'It looks like Strakonis ripped the Flux from its housing and has disrupted the stability of these catacombs. Our presence has disrupted it further… so in short…RUN!!!' cried Lon.

Without a moment to lose, the trio tore
themselves away from the fake Flux and ran as fast
as their legs would carry them back up the windy
catacombs. The heat became unbearable but they
dared not look back.

After a couple of minutes of running flat out, they
burst back onto the surface of the planet and threw
themselves to the ground. A fireball belched
through the hidden door they had just escaped
through.

The tremors began to shake the planet further and
soon the whole planet floor within their vicinity
began to fall in on itself. Lon and the others kept
their heads down as the area shook more and more
violently until, after a minute or so, the earthquake
subsided.

Peering through his arms, Lon looked at the
devastation. As the dust began to settle, Auger and
Etherton helped each other to their feet. Coughing
and spluttering, they joined Lon, who was
overlooking a lip of what now looked like a
mountain.

In the distance emergency sirens were wailing
and getting closer.

The catacombs had been completely destroyed.
Where they once lay was now a precipice that
extended down for hundreds of feet.

Centuries of history wiped out in an instant.

Etherton took off his hat, as if to mourn its
passing.

The sirens were nearly on top of the explorers now.

'Strakonis will pay for what he has done. Just you wait and see,' said Lon through gritted teeth.

'Police! Hands on your heads and get down on the ground. Now!'

The explorers turned to see three squad cars from the Druis security service trapping them against the lip. Armed, chrome-skinned officers pointed large dangerous looking implements in their direction.

They raised their hands in surrender.

'And in the meantime,' said Etherton, 'looks like you'd better write one big cheque to say sorry, Lon!'

II

Random was in trouble. As usual.

In recent times, he had managed to lead a relatively quiet existence, which he had worried would become a frequent pastime for him.

Not long after being born in a giant tube on a war-torn planet he was supposed to be the saviour of, he had found a robot in the shape of a skateboard. Next, having stolen a spaceship from a man made of sand, he crash landed on a little blue and green world in another solar system, where he posed as an orphan in a children's home at the insistence of two teenagers on a school trip. They just so happened to be in the right place at the right time when he nosedived the ship into the planet.

Soon after, he was attacked by the same man made of sand he had stolen the ship from, who had taken over his robot friend and pursued him to the home, which he proceeded to destroy in a fireball.

Not only that, with the help of his new friends and his freed talking skateboard, they then decided that one violent act of criminal damage wasn't enough for one day, so they ended up blowing up the local school and killing the sandman in the process, fleeing before they had the chance to be reprimanded for either!

But at least he had company on his travels. Not only was his talking skateboard back at his side, but the two orphans who found his crashed ship in the woods were also along for the ride. Although, he had some concerns that by allowing them to come along with him, in his travels throughout the cosmos, he might be exposing them to more of the dangers the universe had in store.

He was right.

Their very next adventure was even tougher to recover from than their first.

Random and one of his new friends, a boy called Jake, were incarcerated in the mines of a planet called Genocia, waiting to be fed to a demon from the dark ages of the galaxy, known by the friendly name the Soul Destroyer. The other, a girl called Anji, was lost on the surface of the planet with a band of freedom fighters looking to overthrow a government hell bent on killing its people for profit and power.

So, after experiencing the exciting, thrilling and yet downright dangerous and corrupt ways of the universe, Random was bracing himself for an eventful existence. He needed the distraction.

But since then, not much had happened.

It was a blessed relief for all others concerned. Anji and Jake, after their experiences on Genocia, had taken a little more time to get used to their new life as space explorers.

More time to acclimatise had definitely been needed and thankfully, it's just what they got.

For a few months now the trio, accompanied by their robot Skateboard, had hopped between many of the far corners of the galaxy. They had spent a good while in the effervescent bubble spas of Maltidorn XI, backpacked around the ice honeycombs of Victoliah and discovered a new planet unbeknownst to even Skateboard, with his encyclopaedic knowledge of the cosmos that could sustain life without having a breathable atmosphere.

Along the way…not one abrasive tourist, not one megalomaniac threatening to kill them, no murderous beasts hell bent on ripping them to shreds in the dark cavernous depths of the worst living nightmare possible.

Until now.

It had all started with a letter…

'Anj, what's keeping you? The water's going to get cold again in half an hour.'

Jake hollered for his friend from the relaxing confines of his lilo. He had been lying in the middle of the pool for what seemed like forever, but he wasn't planning to move out of his idea of heaven any time soon. Not even to go to the toilet.

'I'll be there in a minute,' Anji replied as she struggled into her bathing suit. With one final effort, she opened the changing room doors and walked out into the most glorious sunshine the resort had to offer.

The previous day, the explorers' luxury ship, the Venus II, had discovered a moon in the Caloni system which featured a range of free holiday resorts. The resorts were built onto the side of a vast mountain and hung vertically in the air, as gracefully as you'd expect a holiday resort to look when its defying gravity on the side of a sheer drop into oblivion. The view was fantastic, whichever way the holidaymakers looked, and that was enough to blanket the knowledge that the entire complex would end up plummeting down the cliff face if the gravity dampers were to malfunction.

As Anji joined Jake in the pool and the pair began to mingle in the water with other holiday makers, Random sat perched on his sun bed, his chin resting on his hands.

His purple skin glistened in the sunshine. In front of him he could see his friends having the time of their lives. Behind them, the heat of the white dwarf going supernova seven million light years away burnt brighter in his mind than the one that shone on them presently.

He sighed.

He was bored. Very bored.

'Still thinking about the white dwarf, are you sir?'

'Yup.'

Random didn't turn to face the direction the voice had come from. If he had, he'd have seen his faithful friend, Skateboard.

He was perched high up on the sun bed next to
him, a can of oil held up by a claw. A straw rose up
out of the black liquid, surreptitiously leaning into
a cavern where you'd expect a mouth to be.

In better moods, Random would probably have
laughed.

'I'm sure there will be another supernova
sometime soon somewhere,' said Skateboard as he
took another slurp of oil.

'That's pretty presumptuous, old friend.'

'Well, every cloud, as the humans say. You're
restless, aren't you?'

'What gave it away?' said Random sarcastically.

'Well, pretty much everything, sir,' said
Skateboard.

Random sighed again.

'I want adventure, Skateboard. I need adventure!
This kind of thing is okay, every now and then, but
come on! We left Rodas to explore the cosmos.'

'I suppose, an optimist would say that we are
right now.'

'Well, some of us are.' Random's gaze turned to
Anji and Jake. The former, along with two green
headed aliens were having a whale of a time trying
to overturn Jake's lilo.

The shaggy haired blonde was clinging on with
all his might, begging them not to chuck him out
into the water.

'They are new to this, sir.'

'So am I, Skateboard. Okay, yes, it's fine to take a holiday every once in a while, of course it is, but we've had SIX recently! I didn't expect that.'

'Maybe you need to talk with them both. Express your frustration?'

Random turned to his robot and witnessed the crude oil rising from the can and zig-zagging its way up Skateboard's silly straw. He allowed himself a little smile.

'You're right. I'll have a word with them tonight. Hopefully we can move on in the morning.'

'That's a pleasant compromise, sir.'

'That's what I do.'

Skateboard put his can down on the side table, rolled on his hind wheels onto his back and laid settled on the lounger.

There was a question he knew he had to ask, but there was no way he wanted to ask it. Against his better judgment, he decided that now he and his fellow Rodasian were alone, it was the best time.

'Are you still having those nightmares, sir?'

Random's eyes widened.

'Why do you ask?'

'Your welfare, sir.'

Random bowed his head.

'Yes.'

Skateboard's circuitry whirred a little.

'Still the same. "You're the only one who can save your people." "You alone can put a stop to the madness." Y'know, usual thing.'

Back on their home planet of Rodas, the war that had devastated the red/blue planet for centuries continued to rage, divided by two warring factions: the Crimson Empire and the Sapphire Regime. Random was created by rebels from both sides to put a stop to the chaos and save his world from oblivion. But instead of staying and fighting, he had fled and hid and his conscience knew it. Every night since his birth, the same two voices, who by now he had presumed were his parents, had plagued him, urging him home, towards his true calling and his destiny. Still, Random resisted.

'Maybe it's time to go back,' Skateboard asked cautiously.

'No,' Random snapped. 'Not yet.'

'If you wanted me to, I could have a look into your visions myself. Analyse them further. Just to put your mind at ease?'

'It's a kind offer, my friend, but one I'd rather not think about just now.'

Random clicked his tongue and gave a heavy sigh.

'I'll see you back at the Venus.'

He got up from his lounger and walked away from the poolside.

Skateboard was right. He was always right. But to go back now would be suicide. He wasn't ready, not strong enough to face Kalor Maloso again.

He needed more time and yet, the more he thought about Rodas, the more he knew he should be there, putting an end to the suffering.

He was a coward for not doing what he was born to do.

No, not a coward. How could he be? Technically he had saved two planets already, not to mention countless lives so why not Rodas?

He shook the thoughts from his mind as hard as he could.

Random walked towards the docking bay that housed his wondrous ship, the Venus II, and ignored the merry holidaymakers he wandered past, practically oblivious to their existence.

What he needed was another adventure, another distraction.

Thankfully, for him, he got one.

As he rounded the corner, the glorious view of his ship, the Venus II, came into view. Its smooth, silver outline and vast size made it the envy of the docking bay, nay the universe. It was truly a one of a kind.

Random raised a little smile as he saw his home. He'd seen it not a few hours earlier, but every time he gazed upon its magnificence, he was filled with a feeling of reassurance and safety.

'It's you! The purple one!'

Random rounded towards the voice.

A stick thin being, with a nozzle for a mouth and big, oval eyes that blinked out of sync, stood before him, quivering.

'I-I'm so s-sorry. I d-didn't expect y-you to b-be h-here.'

'Where am I supposed to be then?' said Random.

'Ap-pologies. I w-wanted to just leave t-this with your s-ship.'

The being held out its spider-like arms and showed Random what looked like a 3-D realisation of the letter "P".

'Who are you? And what's that?'

'A l-letter.'

'I can see that,' Random tutted. 'What do you want me to do with it?'

'R-return it.'

'To who? And why can't you do it?'

'B-because…the Osirans…t-they b-banished me. I s-stole a v-vital com-p-ponent from them. T-told them I d-did not t-take it. B-but I h-had to. My f-family were s-starving. The Os-sirans took no m-mercy. My b-business w-was g-going under.'

'So, you're only a criminal through desperation, not desire?' said Random.

'N-no. B-but the c-component…it is t-too powerful. I d-did not k-now w-what it w-was. I j-just n-needed the m-money.'

'Hold up a second. So what you are saying is that you want me to take something that was stolen from a race and return it to them?'

The being looked sheepish.

'I-if you can. I-I have h-heard w-what you d-did on Gen-nocia.'

'How?'

'E-everyone has.'

Random looked surprised.

'I suppose news travels quickly in the cosmos.'

'Y-you are heroes.'

'Not us! We won't be signing autographs anytime soon. I don't carry a pen on me, for a start!'

'Y-your humour i-is lost on m-me. P-please. W-will you take it?'

Random huffed. He took the letter from the alien and examined it.

'What is it exactly?'

'I-it is an engine c-component. W-without it, the O-osirans are s-stranded in space.'

'That wasn't very nice of you now, was it?'

'L-like I said. I-I was d-desperate.'

Random glared at the being. It cowered a little further to the ground, the intensity of his red/blue eyes all too much for the thief.

'Supposing I do give it back, who shall I say gave it back to me?'

'O-oh, t-there's n-no need to m-mention my n-name. They w-will know. I-it doesn't m-matter one b-bit who you g-got it from. When t-they g-get it back, you w-will b-be rewarded t-that's f-for sure!'

'I'll have to examine it before I say yes.'

'I-it's not harmful in any w-way, I p-promise.'

Random scoffed. 'Said the criminal who is desperately trying to get rid of it!'

The alien looked forlorn.

'Please…i-it isn't safe for m-me to h-have it. A-and now I k-know I c-can't get anything f-for it, it n-needs to go b-back. I-if I did it, t-they will k-kill m-me for w-what I d-did. I am already r-running from them for my c-crime. T-they have a-agents everywhere. It's n-not safe for me to have i-it and I can't sell it to a-anyone because they k-know w-who it belongs to.'

'So the Osirans…not a friendly bunch then?'

'Y-you'll find out…will y-you d-do it?'

*

'Seriously?' Jake said in disbelief.

'Yep,' replied Random, his arms crossed in staunch defiance.

Jake swung his legs over the side of the lilo and inadvertently splashed Anji, who wore a worried expression.

'So, you want us to leave what I think we can all agree on as paradise to run a dangerous errand for a man who you only just met that could result in certain death? Sign me up!'

'Gotta hand it to you Anj, you're very good at working out the lay of the land!'

Anji scowled at Jake.

'I'm being serious. Random. This isn't a good idea.'

'Look, what's certain death for that alien out there is a picnic for us. We haven't taken the component ourselves. The Osirans will know that. The fella who had it was known to them. We would be greeted as heroes! Again! Yes, I know that might not necessarily be a good thing in the long run, but look, it's a chance to meet a new civilisation. It's an adventure! Come on, it's been ages since we had one. We've got to go!'

'Random, I know you are itching to get back out there. But the Yarvesh…Consula…' Anji shuddered at the memory of both, and the mutts who nearly killed her in the polluted fields of Genocia, 'I was so scared. I could have lost you all for good.'

'I know,' said Random. He sat next to his friend and put a hand upon her shoulder. 'I know how terrified you both were. And I promise I will never put you in such danger again.'

'Then promise us this.' Anji's eyes pleaded with her purple friend. 'Don't put us in danger now.'

A whirring of mechanical instruments emitted from behind them as Skateboard rejoined his friends at the poolside. At the group's insistence, he had been instructed to run a diagnostic on the component, to double check it was not harmful to the travellers.

'I've completed my checks, sir, and I can conclude
that it is nothing more than a fuel cell for an ancient
spaceship. The component is similar to the hydro
fuel cylinders that the Venus II uses to power
herself. Conclusive evidence of danger is zero
percent.'

'That settles it then. Come on you two! Dry off
and let's be on our way!'

Jake rolled his eyes back.

'But we don't even know where to find them!'

'Oh yes we do. The Osirans have been stranded in
the Magidon cluster for four decades in your Earth
terms. We have their coordinates…Please guys.
Look, if it makes you feel any better, you can all sit
this one out and I'll go alone. I need this.
I can't just sit relaxing all the time. There's a whole
galaxy out there to explore…and to be fair I did
warn you from the start that things may get a little
dangerous. It's not like I have done any of it on
purpose.'

Anji put her head in her hands. 'I don't know,
Random. It just feels a little soon.'

'Fine. I'll go by myself then. Skateboard, chuck us
the keys. I'll come and get you all when I am done.'

Jake scrunched his face up.

'Arrg…fine, mate, we'll come along.'

'No, don't worry, if that's really how you feel-'

'-It's okay, I get where you are coming from. I'll
just finish my drink and we'll come along.'

Anji flashed a look of annoyance at her shaggy friend.

'Jake, what are you doing? Reverse psychology won't work. He means it.'

'I think we'd better keep an eye on him Anj, after all, if he never comes back, we'll be stranded here. Besides, he's useless without us.'

Random chuckled. 'That I am.'

Anji took a look around her. The golden glow arced in the atmosphere twinkled with glorious majesty.

'I can think of worse places to be stuck.'

'We can't abandon him. He needs us. Who knows? This time, maybe it won't be as dangerous.'

Anji gave a frustrated cry and wheeled back to Random.

'Alright, Captain, you win. Let's get a wiggle on.'

III

So now, here he was, approaching the throne room of the Osirans with extreme trepidation. The tunnel leading to his destination had been long, dark and dusty, as though it hadn't been used for centuries. Although his mind was clouded by the mystery of the supreme race he was about to meet for the first time, he doubted they had anyone to clean up around the place.

He remembered Skateboard's recon. On the way they had been briefed on exactly who the Osirans were. Supreme gods, legends of the cosmos, who back in the dark ages of the universe had influenced the religious leanings of the ancient Egyptians. Anji and Jake were astonished to learn that the names and stories they had learnt at school were actually true, or at least based on fact.

Despite their newly-found enthusiasm to accompany Random to return the fuel cell, he declined their offer and told them to hang back…and keep the engine ticking over! As he walked out into the grand hall and focused his eyes out of the gloom, he half wished they were with him.

Surrounding him, gazing down from on high, was a multitude of figures sitting still on what looked like sandstone thrones. Random's jaw dropped.

Not only were there dozens of them – hundreds, perhaps – but they towered above him like skyscrapers.

Ten of them, somehow, seemed to dominate the room more than the others, sitting in a circle, like a gladiatorial colosseum. Random soon realised he was standing in what looked like a pit, coarse sand crunching under his feet. He looked nervously around him. Any minute now a giant tiger could leap out from the darkness and try to make him his lunch.

The vast auditorium was silent. An eerie air lingered around him.

He gulped.

Hard.

Remember what Skateboard said, he thought to himself, *speak clearly and with respect.*

'Oh mighty gods...'

Yes, that's a good start, keep going.

'...I am honoured to stand before you today...'

Oh, I'm a natural at this!

'...and I come bearing great news.'

Silence.

Okay, keep going Random.

'My friends and I have reason to believe that we have found something that belongs in your possession.'

Still nothing.

Random frowned a little.

Were these just statues he was talking to? Were they dead? Maybe there was something to do with the fuel cell having shut down?

'A-anyway,' he stuttered, 'I've brought back to you a fuel cylinder…of…erm…great power.'

A loud creak omitted from one of the giants. To Random's amazement, one of the "statues" began to stir into life.

Its body, like its fellow Osirans, resembled that of a human form. Its head differed from the others and looked like that of a bird. If Random could tear his eyes away from it, as its giant beak and moon-like pupils began to peer down on him, he'd have been acutely aware that all of them had differing heads.

'Come closer.'

Its voice boomed throughout the auditorium, a shockwave of vibration disturbing the sand beneath Random's feet. He winced as his ear drums reeled and did what he was asked.

'Show it to us.'

Random produced the fuel cylinder and held it aloft for the Osirans to see.

A huff, loud enough to start an earthquake on a neighbouring planet, emitted from above him.

'Where did you get this?' asked the bird.

'Whom am I addressing?' he dared to ask.

'It is not for me to reveal who I am to someone who we cannot be sure is a friend…or a foe.'

Random decided to chance his wit.

'Well, it would make conversation easier.'

The bird leaned back in its throne.

'I am Horus, god of the Sky.'

Random bowed.

'Delighted to meet you. Blimey, not every day that you meet a god.'

'Gods,' bellowed Horus, 'for we are many.'

Random looked around him and for the first time in quite a while, began to feel slightly afraid.

'All of you?'

'We are many,' boomed another, this time with a longer beak that almost looked like a sword.

'Thoth, please, we are not to entertain this insect,' said Horus.

'Hey! That's a bit strong,' Random protested.

'SILENCE!'

A third voice shrieked from on high. 'The Mother Goddess allows passage within these walls but we shall not tolerate insults towards a stranger.'

'Mother Goddess, we should not take this boy on his word. We must be cautious. After all, was it not an over trust of strangers that led to our crippled state?' said Isis.

'It would be wise to listen to my Mother,' said Horus. 'Would it not, Thoth? Are you or are you not the god of Wisdom?'

'Prey, Horus, do not speak to Thoth on the subject of wisdom. He is wise by title, not by nature. Do you not remember that it was Thoth who allowed us to be robbed of our power in the first place?'

'Hold your tongue, Horus, or I shall have it cut from your mouth!' Thoth shook with indignant rage and forced himself up from his throne. The dust and debris from centuries of dormancy began to fall towards Random.

'Err…did you want to be left alone? I can step outside if now's not a good time.' He thumbed towards the tunnel he came from and failed to notice that it was slowly closing.

'We said silence!' A lightning bolt shot from the raised finger of the Mother Goddess and hurtled towards Random. He rolled forward spectacularly, kicking up a dust cloud as he evaded the strike.

'Woah, woah, what was that for!'

'You have brought the lost fuel cell that will allow our ship to move freely throughout the cosmos once again, but we will not grant you a free pass,' said Osiris.

'You're an accessory to theft and shall be punished.'

'What? I'm here to help you!'

'The Osirans do not require you any further.'

The gods arose from their thrones in unison and raised their arms. As Random turned on his heels, he saw the door was almost shut.

'You will not escape,' boomed Horus.

'Think again,' Random scowled.

Picking up the fuel cell, he moved as fast as he could and squeezed under the descending door, skidding under its crushing weight as the sound of thunder stormed towards him. He had escaped in the nick of time and lost his grip on the fuel cell.

'Ah, nuts!' he exclaimed as he realised he had dropped the cylinder on the other side. He witnessed it separate from him completely as the trap door slammed shut.

Cursing his own theatrical getaway without the possession that had got him into this mess, he made immediately down the tunnel, picking up as much pace as he could muster, tripping as he set off. Even for someone of his immense pace, Random wondered how long it would take him to escape, and indeed if he would even make it out alive at all.

As he hurtled towards freedom, he was becoming aware that he was setting off all manner of traps as he ran. Poisonous darts whizzed past his head, each threatening to put an end to his life one-by-one. He ducked and weaved, and felt a sharp sensation prick his senses into full alert mode when one of the offending weapons whizzed mere millimeters past the worst place to be stung by a dart. Gritting his teeth, he continued on…

Back in the landing bay where the Venus II was parked, Anji and Jake sat on the ships' ramp waiting patiently for their friend to return.

'What's taking him so long?' said Anji, nervously checking her watch.

'Relax. He'll be here in a sec,' Jake reassured.

A distant rumble of activity echoed towards the pair. Jake shot a look as if to say *I told you so* to his friend.

'Anj, you worry too much. He's got it covered. See?'

A purple blur shot out into the hangar, followed by a barrage of explosions.

'Oh, really?' Anji retorted.

'Skateboard!' hollered Jake up the ramp. He scrambled to his feet and followed Anji inside the bowels of the ship. Seconds later, an out of breath, and slightly battered Random joined them, taking out a kitchen cabinet in the mid-section which acted as an unintentional barrier to stop his incredible speed. A tremendous crash of crockery and metal made the occupants of the Venus II's cockpit jump. They looked back into the mid-section just in time to see Random pick himself up and storm towards them.

'I thought I told you to keep the engine ticking over!' he barked, broken bits of crockery hanging like sharp dandruff in his thick brown hair.

'Oh yeah…I stalled it,' said Jake sheepishly.

'You certainly pick your moments to shine, don't you?' he spat, kicking his friend out of the pilot's chair. 'Skateboard?'

'Already on it, sir.'

The AI fired up the motors and the Venus II groaned into life.

Random grabbed hold of the steering column and pulled it towards the ceiling. A volley of laser fire exploded all around the hangar, jolting the passengers forward as it thundered into the craft.

'Shields withholding,' Skateboard announced.

Another crash of fire threw Anji and Jake to the floor and Random and Skateboard from their chairs.

'Shields down,' groaned Random.

He thrust the steering wheel up, catapulting the others to the back of the cockpit. With a roar of agonised Rodasian engineering, the Venus tore out of the hangar and exploded through the blast doors, which had remained shut, into the comforting blackness of space. In all the suddenness of the attack, Skateboard had neglected to think about opening the hangar doors. Even if he had requested it, considering the reception Random had received, he sincerely doubted they would reciprocate with an easier route to freedom.

Even so, he could have thought ahead, anticipated the danger. He could have easily hacked the systems.

The schematics he had researched on the trip to the Osiran mothership had clearly shown him it could be easily done. The ship was ancient, broken, immobilized. Hacking the security system, even that of ancient gods, was as easy to him as it was for a tin opener to make light work of a tin of soup.

But he hadn't, and here they were, running for their lives on a ship that was now damaged.

Anji gingerly got back up to her feet and clung on to the back of Random's pilot chair.

'Anj, Jake, get back to the mid-section now and strap yourselves in.'

She looked to her left. Jake was nowhere to be seen. Anji gasped as she saw the slumped frame of her friend on the ground.

'Jake!'

'Get him out of here now!'

Anji wasn't going to argue with Random. She picked Jake up, struggling under his weight, and dragged him away.

'Sir, the Osirans ship is starting to move.'

'They must have gotten that fuel cell up and running again pretty quickly. Right, priorities. Skateboard, how bad is the damage?'

Skateboard's circuits whirred.

'We've lost shields. Port engine fire is being dealt with by the internal sprinklers and we've almost lost the starboard thrusters all together.'

'Can we outrun the Osirans?'

'For now, sir, yes. But we need to move quickly.'

'Can we go to lightspeed?'

'Negative, sir. If we go to light speed we risk burning the thrusters out completely.'

'Suggestions?'

'We need to find a planet with a breathable atmosphere...'

A deadly array of sparks began to shoot out of the central dashboard.

'Do it!'

Skateboard searched the navigation system.

'Got one. 5 clicks away. Sector 9V4XB.'

Random punched the coordinates into the navigation system.

Anji finished clipping the unconscious Jake into his chair and strapped herself in to hers. She slipped and slid in her place and tried desperately to tighten her bonds but no matter how hard she tried to stay secure, the velocity and buffeting of the broken Venus II was enough to make her sick. More explosions of sparks emitted around the ship, threatening to set the interior of the ship on fire.

Flashes of flames and smoke surrounded the travellers as Random struggled to keep the Venus afloat. The cockpit began to fill with a cloud of smoke.

'Almost there, sir!' Skateboard screamed.

Random peered through the fog in the cockpit and saw a myriad of colours getting ever closer.

He shook his head, wondering whether the fumes he was breathing in was making him hallucinate. Great, that's all he needed during a crash landing!

'Nose up, sir, you've got to keep it up!'

Random's eyes began to feel heavy. His head began to whirl.

'Sir...'

Skateboard pleaded with him to keep focused but it was no use.

As Random slumped off his chair and onto the harsh metal floor, the Venus II spun onto its top.

Skateboard heard Anji scream in the mid-section. Random was down.

The Venus II was on a collision course with a planet…with no one at the wheel…

IV

Skateboard set to work immediately. He was already connected into the ship's steering matrix but it was going to take reactions of lightning quickness to stop the Venus II from plunging into the planet.

He activated the emergency procedure. A safety belt shot out of a gap in Random's chair and anchored his unconscious body firmly to it. He checked his external clock.

0.349 clicks until impact.

There was nothing else he could do except hope, pray to whatever god might be listening and cross his diodes. Even the ones that were hard to reach.

The Venus II had come in hot. Too hot. It smacked into the surface with a terrible force, so great that Anji blacked out almost immediately. The ship bounced with a terrible ferocity across the rocky plane. Sparks flew as the twin engine system on either side of the body of the Venus II turned into huge Catherine wheels of fire.

Inside the spaceship, Skateboard tried all he could to keep the nose up but the gravity of the planet was doing its best to make the crash landing as uncomfortable as possible.

Explosions began to churn like deathly ripples around the place.

Skateboard, already terribly worried by their current predicament, now had fire and three unconscious friends to worry about. Luckily, the sprinkler and foam system kicked in and began to spurt all around him.

Struggle as he might, the ship just would not come to a halt. And then, something terrible happened.

A shriek of metal threw his audio systems into overdrive.

Suddenly Skateboard sensed a harsh breeze blowing in the cockpit.

He dared to look around.

The mid-section had gone.

In the distance, he could just make out the rest of the Venus II as it receded further and further away.

Then, just as he turned back around to face the cockpit view port, his prayers were answered.

The ship has come to a sudden halt.

It had smacked straight into another ship.

This threw the cockpit section of what was left of the Venus II onto its side and finally Skateboard's mission was complete.

Then, just as he thought the day couldn't get any worse, he caused himself a massive embarrassment.

He leaked oil all over the floor and passed out.

'What on Milas was that?!' came a voice from within the vessel that had halted the Venus II's less than glamorous landing.

Three beings clambered out of an opening on the opposite side to the ship. They studied the half a spaceship that had collided with them in complete bemusement.

One of them, the smaller one who resembled what Anji and Jake would know as a mole, rubbed his neck vigorously and looked at the nose cone that had embedded itself in the hull with astonishment and agony.

'What do you think happened?' he said.

The girl, with pale blue skin and hair that seemed to look like an elephant's trunk lying on its side, threw a look at her companion that was dirtier than a ton of manure being dropped from a great height.

'Clearly they crashed, you moron!'

Etherton looked back at her with indignation.

'Ever the wit, aren't you Auger?'

'Shut up, you two,' spat the third member. 'Look.'

He pointed with two of his seven fingers at the smashed window of the cockpit towards the prone body of what looked like a boy.

'Come on,' he gestured.

Lon ran to the other end of the nose cone, closely followed by Auger and Etherton.

'Wait, there's more of the craft over there!' Auger pointed into the middle distance at the rest of the wreckage.

'You two go and check for survivors, quick!'

They obeyed as Lon clambered inside the gutted remains of what until very recently was a mildly tidy cockpit.

He dodged the small fires that were still ablaze and stepped over the debris that lay strewn over what was previously the wall but was now the floor of the craft. He bent down to fit through the door and immediately slipped in the oil that Skateboard had produced before shutting down. Lon's outstretched arms stopped him from hitting his head on the dashboard. He cursed before turning his attention to Random.

Lon winced. The kid looked like he was in a bad way. He checked him for any physical injuries and apart from a gashed arm, which had practically ripped the flesh from the bone, he would live unless he had terrible brain damage.

'Lon?' called a voice from outside the nose cone.

'What is it?' he replied.

Skateboard's circuits began to whirr back into life.

'We've found two more.'

'Get the stretchers out of the ship. I've found one here, and he doesn't look too clever. We'd better bring them on board our ship quickly.'

Skateboard groaned in the way only an AI robot can, startling Lon.

'What are you? What happened?'

Skateboard tried to focus his optical lenses on the stranger who stood over his master's prone body.

Trying to find the words, but unable to while his system continued to boot up, he struggled to produce just three.

'A bumpy landing.'

It was Anji who came around first. As she blinked back into consciousness, a piercing light streamed into her eyes, aggravating an already splitting headache. She emitted a deep, guttural groan and closed her eyes again.

'Ooh, sounds like one of them's back with us,' said Etherton.

He took his feet off his desk and swung himself upright and over to his...patient...he supposed she was.

'Oh, my head!' moaned Anji, placing both her hands against her ears as though there were some terrible earth shattering noise shredding through her brain.

There was.

'Must be concussion or something similar. I don't know, sorry, you've been lumbered with the least medical of our party, I'm afraid. You should have seen the wreck we rescued you from. It's a miracle you aren't dead.'

Anji tried to get up, wincing through the agony.

'No, but your bedside manner clearly is,' she quipped. 'My head...please, do you have anything that will...'

'Oh, yes, hold on a second,' the mole-like creature scurried around what Anji presumed was the medical bay. It was certainly bright enough to resemble one.

'Could you turn the light down too?'

'Hold on, I only have one pair of paws!'

Finally, he grabbed a sachet of liquid, tore the corner slightly and handed it to Anji.

'Take a few swigs of that, should sort you right out.'

She did as instructed and instantly her headache began to subside. Anji began to sit up straight and forced her eyes fully open. No longer shrouded by pain, she took in her surroundings.

'Is this a hospital?'

Etherton snorted. 'Hah! Far from it.'

'Then where am I then?'

Suddenly her eyes shot wide when she realised she was alone.

'Oh my god, Jake and Random!'

She tried to get to her feet but was gently pushed back onto the bed by the strange alien who had saved her from potential death by headache.

'Please, little lady, you have to remain still. The drugs won't have fully worn off yet.'

The mention of drugs began to make Anji panic.

'You've drugged me!? Get off me!'

'No, no not like that! Please miss, stop struggling!'

'What the hell do you think you are doing?'

Auger had entered the room and as usual was shaking her head in dismay at her travelling companion.

'You've never been very adept at talking to women, have you Etherton?' she snorted, pulling him away.

Auger could see the panic in Anji's eyes.

'You and your friends are safe, now please take it easy.'

'Where are they?' Anji demanded.

'They are right next door.'

'Can I see them?'

'Of course – just as soon as you have fully recovered.'

'Why? What happened?'

'You don't remember?' asked Etherton.

Anji searched her memory. Of course she did. The Osirans. The ship was gunned down. They had crashed!

'I do, oh my…' she caught her breath. 'Are they alright?'

'They will be, now.'

Another voice had entered the room.

Anji surveyed the newcomer.

He stood a proud six feet tall, with thick black wavy hair floating down his short forehead and over his left eye. His arms were muscular with his biceps popping out from underneath his sleeveless jacket and Anji noticed that he had seven fingers on each hand…and there were three of them!

Whoever he was, he was definitely the best looking alien Anji had ever seen.

'Now? What happened to them?'

'Let's just say that you were in much better shape than them.'

Anji gasped.

'I'll let you see them just as long as the drugs have passed out of your system.'

'What drugs?'

'Trauma supplements. You and your friends have been through hell by the looks of it.'

Lon dragged a chair across the room to Anji's bed.

'Now, why don't you tell me what happened to you and your friends while we wait for them to wake up?'

Anji fell silent. She was unsure what to say. Should she mention the Osirans? Were these people good guys? Could she trust them?

'We had engine failure and just happened to crash land.'

'Emphasis on the crash and less on the land, I'd say,' butted Etherton.

'Etherton, hush,' said Auger.

'Well, how do you expect me to feel? Her ship took out my living quarters!'

'Took out? Oh no, we didn't crash into you, did we?'

'Crashed?! You put a hole in our ship!'

Anji began to feel a little awkward.

'Didn't you see us coming?'

Auger laughed. 'We were parked!'

Anji blushed.

'Sorry.'

Lon smirked. 'Don't worry about them, we'll fix it. Are you sure it was engine failure? We've surveyed the wreckage and there were what looked like scorch marks on the hull.'

'Well we were on fire…from what I remember…' Anji said, rubbing her head.

'I wasn't born yesterday. It was from laser fire. So come on, tell us, what really happened?'

'What's going on in here?'

Yet another new voice entered the makeshift medical bay.

Lon, Auger, Etherton and Anji turned around in unison and couldn't help but look deeply shocked at their visitor. Instantly they all shot their gaze away again.

'What's your friend's name again?' said Lon.

'Jake! What are you doing?' Anji sounded embarrassed.

'Why, what's the matter?' said Jake.

'Jake is it? I take it he isn't very clever,' said Etherton.

'Hey! That's a bit personal, you haven't even met me properly yet!'

'That's my fault, sorry,' admitted Auger.

'Right, well take him back to the main medical bay,' demanded Lon, 'And for god's sake put his surgical gown on the right way around this time!'

V

A few hours later, the crew of the Venus II were almost as good as new, having recovered from their injuries. Along with those who had rescued them, they congregated in a meeting area of Lon's ship.

Random slurped the last of his revitalizing tonic and replaced the cup on the table they were sat around.

'Thanks for that, it really was a lifesaver.'

'You're not kidding. Always handy to keep around in our line of work.'

'What is it you do?' asked Jake, who was over his embarrassment from earlier and had also fully recovered from his injuries. When he was found by Auger and Etherton, his body was broken in so many places the pair had severely doubted he would make it back to their ship alive. Despite their lack of optimism, he did, and after they had delicately managed to zip both he and the others into bio suits, designed to help regenerate damaged body tissue, and pumped him and his friends full of trauma supplements, he had made a full recovery in a matter of hours.

'We're archaeologists. We travel the cosmos looking for rare and sometimes mythical artifacts, find them and sell them,' said Auger.

'Sounds amazing! I've always wanted to be an archaeologist,' said Jake.

'No you haven't, you've always wanted to be a footballer,' Anji retorted.

'Well…' said Jake, slightly embarrassed, '…that's what I tell people to look cool.'

'Anyway, what are you doing here…and where is here anywhere?' asked Random, trying to steer the conversation back on course.

'Before we answer any more questions,' said Etherton, 'I think it's only fair you tell us who you are running from.'

'Oh, no-one at all. We got caught in the crossfire of a little space skirmish, that's all.'

Lon searched Random's face for any hint of a lie. He found none.

Random was a very good liar.

'That's as well because if anyone were to find out what we are doing here, they'd probably end up firing on us too.'

'How come?' asked Anji.

'We are here to find the Zedron Flux.'

'Never heard of it,' said Jake.

'I'm very surprised at that. Where are you from?' Auger was astonished. Everybody in the universe had heard of the Zedron Flux.

'Well, let's just say we travel a lot and don't really belong anywhere,' said Anji. Jake shot her a look.

'That's a bit on the nose, Anj, everyone belongs somewhere,' he replied.

'That's what we like to think,' she said.

'The Zedron Flux is pure energy. Used correctly it can be the one thing that can save the universe from all its ills.'

'Sounds a bit grand. How come it needs finding, something that strong?' said Random.

'It doesn't. It was stolen,' said Auger.

'Stolen? From who?' asked Anji.

'From me,' said Lon bitterly.

'From us,' Auger corrected. Lon shot a dirty look at his counterpart.

'Who pays you, Auger?' he continued.

The explorer bit her lip.

'And the person…or people who took it from you, there here on this planet?' asked Random.

'Yes, and hopefully so is the Flux,' said Lon.

Random clapped his hands and got to his feet. 'Well, we don't want to bother you any longer than we have, come along you two.'

Lon laughed. 'Where exactly? We haven't even told you where you are. Besides, you left us with a hole in our hull and we could use some extra pairs of hands.'

'We don't want any trouble,' said Random firmly.

'You won't get any. Don't worry, we'll look after you.'

'We don't need any looking after.'

'If you say so. But you've left us with heavy damage. It would only be fair if you repaid us in kind.

So what do you say? Wanna join us on a treasure hunt?'

'Yes please!' said Jake.

'We all know you do, Jake,' tutted Anji.

'As long as we stay safe,' said Random.

'I can't guarantee that, but we can do our best,' replied Lon.

'We'd better speak to Skateboard first, see how the Venus II is doing.'

'There's little point in that. From the mess your craft was in I doubt it will ever fly again,' chuckled Etherton.

At that moment Skateboard slid into view.

'Self-repair mode is currently at 38 percent. According to early diagnostic tests she'll fly again, sir,' he chirped.

'Good,' Random smirked cheekily in Etherton's direction.

'It'll take quite a while for the Venus II to pull itself all back together again. We could be here for days, weeks even,' Skateboard informed.

'It looks like you have no choice but to join us then,' said Lon.

'Yes…but it would be nice to know where we are exactly.'

Lon made for a side door and pressed the release mechanism.

A blaze of colours bled into the ship.

'Welcome to Spectronia.'

The travellers gazed in sheer wonder at the mass of sheer beauty that surrounded them. They all cooed at the wondrous collection of rainbows that were painted across the clear blue sky. Rolling mountains surrounded them, each one coated in a wash of all the colours of the spectrum. Random's eyes glimmered as he gazed at the shimmering mountain tops, the snow a glistening drift of multi-coloured glory.

'Are we in heaven?' cooed Anji.

'This is…I mean, wow!'

'Couldn't have put it better myself, Jake,' said Random.

'Every colour imaginable!' squeaked Anji.

'Yes. It's a pity there were no rainbows on Rodas,' mused Random as he spotted a purple colour matching that of his pigmentation all around him. 'There would never have been a war in the first place.'

'Your people went to war over colour? Seems a little senseless to me,' said Jake.

'Says a human,' Random replied.

'Fair point.'

Jake went back to concentrating on the beautiful view. He thought back to his days at primary school, when he and his fellow classmates would play with rainbow crayons. It was as though someone had gone to town on the whole planet with a lorry load of them.

The horizon glistened in the sunshine, which seemed to resemble the one back in Anji and Jake's solar system.

Random tried to tear his attention away from the wonder and to the task in hand.

'How long have you been here?'

'About two days,' said Auger.

'Do you ever plan to leave?' asked Anji.

'As soon as we have the Flux,' said Lon, who began to rummage through his backpack.

'But surely people of your occupation can take huge pleasure being in a place as gorgeous as this?' said Anji.

'Oh yes, I agree!' said Etherton. 'After all, Spectronia is one of the nine wonders of the galaxy. Picturesque, peaceful, majestic in all of its splendour. The trouble is Lon is such a grump he refuses to take it all in!'

Lon glared at Etherton, enough to make him nervous. 'A-anyway, would you like some warmer clothes? Spectronia can get quite cold at night.'

'We should have some on board the Venus II, thanks,' said Random. 'Come on gang, let's tool up. How long before you wanted to get on the road, as it were?'

'What road?' said a bemused Auger.

'It's an Earth phrase. Blimey, you two must have rubbed off on me more than I realised…see!' He grinned at his two human counterparts. 'What time shall we meet you back here?'

'You're crashed vessel isn't far away, just be as quick as you can,' said Lon.

The trio, led by Skateboard, made the small journey on foot towards the shipwreck.

To the naked eye, the ship looked in a terrible state, beyond repair. Shards of metal and debris lay a path guiding the travellers closer and closer to the ruin.

The Venus II was still torn in two, but there appeared to be a blue energy glowing around the rim of the nose section, pulling it very slowly towards the rest of the craft. Jake noticed the sound of metal being hauled together and hydraulics somewhere from within the ship, working overtime. It sounded like a building site.

'Alright, Skateboard, full damage report please,' asked Random.

'Um…it's dead!'

'Far from it, Master Jake,' insisted Skateboard. 'The Venus II is equipped with a self-repair mechanism powered by microscopic organisms manufactured in the seda metal. In other words, unless it is completely unsalvageable, it'll always pull itself back together. Although it has to be said that this was a close call.'

'We're a lucky bunch!' chirped Anji. 'Random, I'm not sure about those three. They seem…cold.'

'I know what you mean. Especially that Lon fella.

I think we should try and keep our wits about us on this trip, just in case.'

'Well we could always just stay with the Venus II?' said Jake, cautious all of a sudden.

'And miss this chance to explore one of the nine wonders of the galaxy?' exclaimed Random, who was now aching for adventure again.

'Come on Jake, like Random said, as long as we stay on our toes there's nothing to worry about. Also, you heard Skateboard back at their ship. It could take days for the Venus to repair herself.' Anji said.

'Maybe even a week or two,' Skateboard confirmed.

'Exactly.'

'Also, the self-repair system would make the Venus II quite uninhabitable until it is finished.' Skateboard continued.

'But who will look after it? I mean, who knows what kind of monsters might be lurking around the next rainbow?' asked Jake.

'He's got a point, Random,' said Anji.

Random looked at Skateboard.

'During the main reconstructive phase of the rebuild the outer hull of the ship will be sending electrical pulses throughout. Meaning it would be impossible for anyone to get close to it...'

'...and keep their face in the process?' said Random.

'Eloquently put, sir,' said Skateboard.

'How long until this…phase starts?' asked Anji.

'As soon as we are ready to leave. Remember I am connected to the ship. I can initialize any command or override remotely.'

'Just like a set of car keys, you can make sure the riff raff are locked out,' said Jake.

'Precisely.'

'Well then, we'd better not lose our keys then,' joked Random. 'Come on you lot, let's get packing.

VI

For such a sunny day, Anji expected the heat to bake them as they continued in the open top buggy. Yet somehow, the temperature on Spectronia was more than adequate for them. Not too hot, not too cold. In a word, it was perfect. Just what she thought the planet was too.

Deep down she had been more than skeptical about going on another adventure so soon after the crash. But whatever Lon and the others had given them had certainly worked. She didn't feel any after effects of the accident at all. Which was weird for someone who just a few hours previously had broken all of her limbs, suffered a major spinal shattering and to top that all off, had a splitting headache.

Although their new friends had confirmed that she had got off better than the other two, she hadn't wanted to enquire what had happened to them. That kind of information could really put someone off their tea.

Now here they were, sitting in the back of a dune buggy holding on for dear life as the sun shone its warm rays down upon them.

It wasn't the coziest of rides, but it was a damn sight comfier than their crash landing!

Back at Lon's ship, Random had asked how they were planning to track down the Flux.

'With this,' Auger had answered, brandishing a device which looked like a cross between a fish fork and a TV remote. 'It's an energy locator. When the Flux is near, energy will spike. So far, we have determined that it is roughly 200 miles southwest of our location.

'200 miles? In space terms that's, what? Ten minutes away? Right, Skateboard?' said Jake.

'It does seem like a very short trip,' said Skateboard.

'On the contrary. We weren't joking when we said this was a long trip,' said Lon. 'We've been tracking it for the best part of seven months. Unfortunately, the person who is holding it to ransom has detected us on every occasion. Why? Because of this thing. He's able to detect our vessel from a distance. So, this time, we have to be cunning, take him by surprise and take what should be mine.'

'Ours,' corrected Etherton.

''I know what I mean,' spat Lon. 'Now come on, before he moves again.'

So now here they were, in the back of the buggy, no seatbelts, holding on for dear life as it negotiated its way up the sand dunes.

'Is there any way this could go a little…slower?' said Jake. The steep inclines and falling declines were making his teeth chatter and his cheeks wobble.

He wasn't the only one. Looking over at Random, Jake could see nothing but a purple blur.

'Fraid' not. We are making good time.'

'Any chance we can get on a smoother road? Those rainbow roads look nice!' shouted Anji over the loud buggy's engine.

Jake leant closer to Random.

'Not being funny, mate, but it's making me numb.'

'I don't think our driver wants to, sorry, I'm not the Captain here.'

Jake huffed.

'According to the map, the route should level out soon,' Etherton said, emerging from underneath what looked like a large duvet.

'Told you you should have gone digital, Etherton,' joked Auger.

'Hey, when you're navigator, do what you want, but when I'm in charge-'

The buggy came to a sudden halt, hurling its incumbents forward. Anji nearly hit her head on the back of Auger's seat. She caught a glimpse of Lon's expression in the rear-view mirror. He did not look happy.

'Will you all, please, for one minute just keep your mouths closed?'

The car fell silent.

'Thank you,' Lon huffed.

Skateboard was lying across the laps of his

companions as there was little space in the buggy
for a seventh person.

He started to whir.

'Er…sorry to break the silence…'

'Not as much as I am,' Lon interrupted.

'But I am picking up life forms on the mid-range
scanner.'

The crew of the dune buggy looked around, alert
to danger.

'How many, Skateboard?' asked Random.

'Roughly 60…no 70…80…I'll get back to you on
that figure, sir!'

'I'm swinging this buggy round,' Lon declared.

Random got out of the buggy and walked up the
dune to get a better look. His eyes widened.

'Wait, we don't know if they are hostile,' said
Anji.

'We're about to find out,' said Random
ominously.

On the horizon was a stampede of beings,
seemingly riding on the backs of other creatures.
They were still a little too far out for Random to see
any more than this except that they each appeared
to have some form of weapon on them…and they
looked sharp.

'Get in the car!' hollered Lon.

He ticked the engine over and grappled with the
steering wheel, swinging the car one hundred and
eighty degrees. Random jumped gracefully into the
back of the buggy, panicked.

'Drive.'

The buggy tore away from the oncoming threat and kicked up a cloud of sand and dust in its wake. Random, Anji and Jake kept their heads turned towards the chaos. The creatures had already gained so much ground that they were closer to them than they were to escaping.

Much closer.

The beasts pursued them with relentless intent and Anji cried in terror whenever she was able to see them clearly through the dust cloud. They looked to her like black horses. Five legged horses, with one in the middle of the front two, each with what looked like hooves made of spears, just as pointy as the colourful jockeys who rode upon them.

A sharp object was hurled towards the buggy and Random used his super speed abilities to intercept it and pluck it out of the air.

'Do that again and I'll buy you a drink!' said Lon.

'I'm not old enough to drink!'' Random replied, instantly regretting his response and relegating it to the least cool thing he had ever said during a chase.

'Incoming!' yelled Jake.

A spread of spears hit the back of the buggy and one embedded itself in the seat where Random had been sitting.

'Leave this to me, Anj, Jake, keep down!'

'Their almost on top of us, Lon! Hurry!' cried Auger.

Splinters and shards of weaponry flew above them. Despite Random's best efforts a pile of debris was starting to collect in the foot wells beneath Jake and Anji's feet. Seeing their predicament as a chance to be heroic and impress their new friends, Jake picked up one of the broken spears and stood up from his seat, brandishing it and gritting his teeth in a "come and have a go if you think you're hard enough pose".

Within seconds, it had been knocked out of his hand by the precise throw of an identical spear and with a whimper, he sat quietly down.

'Get down!' said Random, his concentration being distracted long enough for another sharp weapon to fly into the vehicle.

'We can't outrun them!' said Etherton.

'Yeah, I don't need a running commentary, people!' shouted Lon angrily.

But his mole-like friend was not wrong. They were almost outrun. Lon was not in control of the situation. He hated it when this happened…and it wasn't often that he felt like this.

The buggy continued to lurch up and down the sand dunes at breakneck speed and yet it was all but surrounded now.

Whoever, whatever were following them began to try to climb on board the buggy, but Random, helped by Anji and Auger, tried with all his might to throw the uninvited guests off their vehicle. But it was becoming impossible.

'It's no use,' cried Random as he struggled with five of them.

Giving into the chase, Lon reluctantly began to slow the vehicle down.

The buggy came to a sad, inevitable stop.

Amazingly, the natives began to climb down. Jake dared to open his eyes and gaze through the cracks in his fingers. The hunting pack had circled them. There was no way out.

The beasts whinnied exactly in the way that horses don't as they reared and thundered to a halt.

The explorers looked around them. There must have been a hundred of the creatures.

Instinctively, they all put their hands up.

'Okay, we don't want any trouble,' said Lon.

Silence.

'We come in peace,' said Random.

'You don't get to do the talking here,' spat Lon.

'Do you think this is a good time to argue?' replied Random.

A female voice came forth from the hoard.

'Who among you is the leader of your tribe?'

'I am,' said Random and Lon at the same time.

The circle parted a little. From the void, a warrior rode forward, wearing a crown that looked like a collection of pan pipes.

'How can this be? There can only be one who makes decisions for your tribe.'

'We're a committee,' said Random. 'Who, may I ask, is addressing us?'

'Very formal,' Anji muttered.

'You are trespassing in our territory. Trespassing is punishable with incarceration.'

'I'm sorry. We didn't know. We were following a trail and it led us through here. Believe me, we did not mean to intrude,' said Random.

'Who are you?' asked Anji.

'I am Solenia. Ruler of the Spectronians.'

'What are they saying?' asked Auger.

'Of course,' exclaimed Random. He turned to his friends. 'Remember the translation capabilities of the Venus II? It must be working. That's why we know what the Spectronians are saying but the others don't!'

'And why we can understand Lon and the others too,' said Anji.

'Not a clue,' said Etherton, answering Auger's original question.

'Pleased to meet you, Solenia,' replied Lon.

Random looked at the explorer curiously.

'You speak Spectronian?'

'You pick up all kinds of languages when you've been to as many places as I have,' said Lon.

'You are strangers here. We cannot allow the peoples of this world to roam our plains without gaining our approval first.'

Jake gazed at Solenia with teenage lust. She had long, flowing, golden locks and a body that he had only seen in movies. True, she also looked like she had bathed in a rainbow fountain, her skin just as vibrant as the rest of this amazing planet. Indeed, had it not been for the strange alien horses they appeared to be riding, Jake was certain he wouldn't have seen her at all…except for that glorious hair. Her spectrum skin made for an almost perfect camouflage against all else on the unique landscape.

Anji looked over and noticed that Jake had a vacant look in his eye…far vaguer than that he usually possessed, and immediately thought it inappropriate to laugh.

'We mean you no harm,' Random assured her.

'Then why do you come here to Spectron?'

'Spectron? I thought this planet was called Spectronia?'

'That is what the non-we call it. Only true natives of Spectron call this great planet by her correct name. Now I shall ask you again: why do you come here?'

'I can't tell you,' replied Lon.

Solenia and her warriors raised their spears.

'Woah, woah, woah, there's no need for that!' said Random.

'I've come a long way. I'm not giving away our intent,' Lon said in a hushed tone towards him. 'We do come in peace though, I assure you.'

Solenia's eyes narrowed.

'You come with us.'

'I'm afraid we cannot,' Lon argued.

'You come with us!' Solenia repeated forcefully.

Lon exhaled.

'Yeah, let's go with her,' Jake dribbled.

Anji shot a look of disapproval at him.

'Do what they say,' Random urged Lon.

Lon growled in anger and sat back in his seat.

The circle began to move forward, the beasts maintaining their formation around the captured explorers, like travellers surrounded by Indians in the Wild West.

'Random? What are we going to do?' asked Anji.

'I'm sure we'll work something out,' he smiled, placing a reassuring hand on her arm.

Anji's eyes were a pool of worry.

Random hid his by closing them.

VII

Random's arms were going dead. He looked up at them as they dangled from the wall.

Try as he might to wiggle them back into life, the manacles were too tight around his wrists.

He huffed and looked at his fellow captives.

Anji and Jake looked thoroughly fed up. Auger had spent the last two hours pulling at her restraints and was still convinced she could snap them from the wall.

Etherton looked sad, scared for he and his counterparts' immediate future.

Lon just sat there, a steely expression of cold determination washed over his face.

'They are going to eat us, I'm sure of it!' cried Etherton.

'If they do then I hope I'm the starter. I don't think I could stomach seeing you lot being served up on a platter,' said Anji.

'How's Skateboard holding up?' asked Jake.

Anji looked to her left to check on their AI robot. He was in a hell of a state.

The Spectronians had clamped him down in a contraption that resembled a vice and had placed a magnet on his back, incapacitating his circuitry so he was less likely to hatch an escape plan.

For a seemingly primitive race, they are technologically knowledgeable, he had thought as the magnet had been placed on his back by the guard and his voice box became as scrambled as eggs.

'DWATERFUNGERNUFF,' he waffled.

'Did anyone get that?' Jake asked hopefully.

'Yes, it means, "shut up everyone, I'm trying to think!"' snapped Lon.

Random scowled.

'You may be angry, Lon, but snapping at my friend won't get you out of here.'

'Oh yeah, what will then?'

'Telling them what they want to know would help.'

Lon spat on the floor. 'I'd rather die than give them any advantage over me.'

'What advantage?' asked Anji.

'The Flux of course! If we tell them what we are here for then it's highly conceivable that they will leave us to rot in here and go get it for themselves.'

'Well, what if they did? You could always break out and take it back then? In a way they'd be doing your dirty work,' Random pointed out.

'No one, no one, but me are getting their disgusting hands on the Flux!'

Anji looked over at Etherton.

'Has he always been like this?'

'Ever since we lost the Flux, yes.'

'Well, he must pay well.'

'What makes you say that?'

Anji raised her eyebrows.

'I can't see why you'd still be with him if he didn't.'

Lon glared at Anji. If looks could kill, she'd have been dead instantly.

'Anji,' Random tried to temper his friend. 'Antagonising one another isn't going to help things. I'm getting a bit fed up with hanging around myself but we have to think of the positives.'

'Such as?' asked Auger, finally taking a break from her efforts.

'Such as, if we can get the Spectronians on our side, reason with them, we might be able to get the Flux back quicker than we expected.'

'And how do you propose we do that?' said Lon.

'By talking and being civil.'

'Ha!' cried Lon.

'Well then, let me have a go. Maybe I can reason with her.'

'No.'

'Lon.'

'You're a child.'

'Random's much more than that,' said Anji. 'You think you are the only one who's keeping secrets? If we told you what we have done in the past you'd start to take us a little more seriously.'

Lon's fists unclenched.

'Go on them enlighten me.'

'Not until you tell us who's got the Flux currently,' said Random.

'No.'

'Why not?'

'Because it's nothing to do with you, that's why.'

'We are risking our lives here Lon, for goodness sake, give us that at least!' Random was starting to lose patience with him.

'Strakonis,' said a voice.

Lon looked over in Auger's direction.

'Traitor!' Lon whispered to himself, loud enough for everyone to hear. Auger inhaled sharply. The word was like a knife in her back.

'Whose Strakonis?' asked Anji.

'Come on, everyone knows who Rogar Strakonis is,' said Etherton.

'Well we don't,' said Jake.

Auger continued. 'Rogar Strakonis is known throughout the galaxy as one of the richest explorers in the twelve belt system.

For years he and Lon have fought, testing one another, racing against themselves to find the treasures of the cosmos.'

'In short then, he's a rival,' affirmed Random.

'More than that,' said Lon. 'Strakonis has used his wealth to buy real estate in the twelve belt system.'

'What's that when it's at home? asked Jake.

'A ribbon of planets hanging in twelve rows in the stars.

Strakonis has taken over half of that sector of space, built his empire of wealth on selling the land.'

'So he's a sort of intergalactic landlord?' asked Anji.

'It's a little more complicated than that,' said Lon.

Before he could continue his story, the dungeon gates swung open. An impossibly tall warrior stood with a weapon in hand in the doorway.

'You. Come.'

The warrior was pointing at Random.

'Oh alright, if you insist.'

The prison guard, key in hand, made for Random's manacles. Deep down, Random knew that he could snap them as easy as a child could a twig. That's one of the advantages of having super strength.

Luckily, neither Anji or Jake had given that fact away.

Judging by their moods, he guessed that they knew that he was buying time for something. But then what would he have learnt of the explorers he and his friends had aligned themselves with if he hadn't? But he had wanted to know what Lon was really up to.

There was something fishy about the three of them, and now he was getting close to the real reason of Lon's secrecy. But then why didn't he want to tell them the full story in the first place? He'd have to find out.

But first, he had to make sure he could bargain for their freedom.

Solenia heard the knocking from the other end of the courtroom. She took her time making her way back to her throne, resplendent in gold and burgundy materials, flanked either side by guards and two handmaidens. Sitting down, she beckoned the two footmen at the door to allow her prisoner to enter. As the long doors creaked open, Random, accompanied by two spear wielding guards, made his way of the long rainbow coloured gangway to the throne.

'Lovely place you've got here,' he said. 'You should see where they have put us up!'

Solenia smiled.

'A cheeky one. Very brave too.'

'Well, I try my best,' he smiled. Random looked above him. A glorious diamond window hung high above them, the sun blazing through and washing the courtroom with its brilliant rays.

'Tell you what, after you threw us in that dungeon I was beginning to think that I'd never get to see the sun again.'

'It clearly is not yours judging by the colour of your skin.'

'Oh, no one should be judged by the colour of their skin,' he retorted.

'And yet many do. We've had visitors from other worlds here before. None so much like you.

Each and every one of them threatened to disrupt the peace that we fight so hard to retain on Spectron.'

'Can't be a lot of peace if you are fighting,' said Random. He nodded at the spears. 'I mean, these can't be just for decoration, can they?'

'We are at liberty to protect ourselves. Show me a Queen who does not protect her subjects and I'll show you a broken world.'

Random smiled at her with appreciation.

'I wanted you brought to me as I thought I may get answers from you. You seem different to the others in your party.'

'I am. Myself and the two humans crash landed here and were rescued by Lon and the others.'

'What caused this accident?'

Random thought hard and fast to hide the truth. If this truly were a planet enduring to keep the peace from alien visitors, how could he tell the ruler of it that they were on the run from Egyptian gods, who if they were unlucky could turn up at any moment and blow the planet up? In that split second, he believed that the truth was not what Solenia needed to hear right now.

'An engine malfunction in our ship. Our AI robot has managed to fix the fault and within a few days we should be able to leave again.'

'If you are allowed to leave my custody, that is.'

Random blinked.

'Yeah, good point.'

'What is your name?'

'Random.'

'Random. My people are great in number but we prefer to live a life in the shadows. We do not ask for the attention of others, nor do we seek the treasures that I am sure your companion Lon desires. However, my main priority for all is the safety of my subjects. I suspect that your friend has come in search of another here on our world.'

'I believe so,' said Random.

'Answer me this truthfully, purple one, is this stranger likely to be a threat to us here on Spectronia?'

'It's hard to say,' said Random honestly. 'I believe there is a rivalry between said person and Lon. Whether it's a violent one, I don't think so. But it's clear to me he has something that belongs in Lon's possession. If you could let us go, not only can I keep my eye on Lon, but I reckon we could make sure that this Strakonis fella also leaves this planet well alone.'

Solenia's ears seemed to prick up at the mention of Strakonis' name.

'Oh?' said Solenia. 'How so?'

'Well, if Lon takes back what he believes is his he certainly won't hang around Spectronia...sorry, Spectron, to lose it again.'

Solenia got up and stood in front of Random.

He stood at the foot of a row of steps leading up to her. She towered over him, looking down but not lowering her head to meet his gaze.

'This…thing, he is in possession of. Is it a weapon?'

'In the wrong hands, it could be.'

She reeled.

'Then we must not let the prospect of conflict linger.'

Solenia sat calmly back on her throne.

'Random, I shall give you your freedom, on one condition.'

Random bowed. 'Thank you, your grace. What can I do in return?'

'There is more to you than meets the eye. I can sense it. A great power resides within you. If you can prove my senses true, then I am fully confident that you can guide Lon to finding what he has lost and in doing so, ensuring that this… Strakonis, as you call him, is also detained and taken away from this planet. Are you up to this task?'

'Saving worlds and stopping the bad guys? It's almost a hobby of mine.'

'Then go. I shall see to it that your friends are also set free. My chief architect can help you find easier routes to any journey you may need to take.'

'That's great news, thank you, your grace.'

Random bowed again and turned for the door.

'And Random?'

He stopped and faced Solenia.

'Go well.'

VIII

Before long, Anji, Jake, Lon, Auger and Etherton had been released from their prison and joined Random in the throne room. Not that they were very grateful for it, especially Anji.

'So why couldn't you do your usual kick-ass routine and get us out of there?' she whispered in hush tones as the group waited for the Chief Architect to arrive.

'Because I wanted to find out what that lot were up to,' he whispered back, gesturing quietly towards Lon and his companions.

'But did you have to leave us chained up for so long?' butted in Jake.

'Alright, I'm sorry I couldn't get us out of there sooner. But we need to know what kind of people we are dealing with here. Something tells me they aren't your average archaeologists.'

'Yeah, they're space ones!' said Anji.

'No, there's something else. Don't you feel it?'

Random knelt down towards Skateboard, who was busying himself scanning the area.

'Skateboard, found out anything interesting?'

'Yes, sir. It appears the Spectronians live underground. This throne room is roughly four hundred metres under the planet's surface.'

'How?' said Lon, overhearing the conversation.

'We didn't go down even a flight of stairs!' said Etherton. 'I think your robot might be broken.'

'I can assure you my diodes are functioning perfectly,' Skateboard replied. 'The tunnels are submerged but oxygen is filtered down here by air vents in the sand.'

'I'm surprised they don't get clogged!' said Anji.

'How did we get under here if none of us noticed we were going underground?' asked Random.

'The tunnels act on a pivot. As weight is transferred, the corridors at the entrance tip, but gravity keeps those walking towards the other end upright, replicating a normal experience.'

'Sounds cool!' said Jake.

'So how do we get out?' asked Auger.

At that moment, the Chief Architect arrived in the throne room, armed with rolls upon rolls of parchment paper. His head was the shape of light bulb, only fifty times bigger, and like everyone else on this Spectronia, his skin was all the colours of the rainbow.

'So, so sorry to have kept you all,' he said in a flustered tone as he tried to clear space on a small table. 'Oh! Wow! Aliens!'

'What did he call me?' said Auger.

'I know right?' said Jake.

'No, genuinely, it's starting to grate not being able to understand anyone on this crazy planet.'

'I've never seen real life aliens before! I mean obviously there's other beings in this universe, but to actually be standing in the same room as them. Wait until I tell the kids!'

Random offered his hand.

'Random.'

'Yes, isn't it!' the Architect enthused. 'Possil's the name.'

Anji stepped forward. 'Anji's mine, this is Jake, Skateboard and Random.'

'Oh!' I do apologise.' He scuttled over to Lon.

'And you are?'

Lon stared at him unmoved.

Possil's smile ebbed away.

'Right. Anyway our great ruler has informed me that you would like to see plans of the area?'

'A little more than that,' said Lon. 'We are looking for stolen goods and every second we waste with pleasantries the further it gets away.'

'I'm sorry Mr Possil, please try to ignore him, incarceration has stoked his already foul mood,' said Random quietly. 'Any help you can offer us is greatly appreciated.'

Possil regained his smile. He unfurled one of the huge parchments and used the others to keep either side from folding back in on themselves and beckoned the travellers to the table.

'This is the Western Seam of Spectronia.'

'That's more like it,' Lon's interest was well and truly peaked. 'This is where we need to go.'

Anji ran her eyes over the crude drawings.

'Looks a bit rocky to me.'

'It is, miss. You'll have to go easy along the mountain sides. But as soon as you reach the pinnacle you can get on one of the roads and it should make for a better journey.'

'Skateboard, could you scan these images?'

'Certainly, sir.' A small blue light began to swipe over the map.

Jake scratched his messy blonde hair. 'But these maps look ancient; won't the landscape have changed since they were made?'

'Jake's got a point, do you have anything a little more up-to-date?' asked Random.

'These maps may have been commissioned by our founding Mothers and Fathers twenty centuries ago, but the landscape has not changed in that time,' said Possil.

'What? Not even through climate change?' asked Jake.

'Climate what?' enquired Possil.

'You're all babbling again,' snapped Lon. 'What is the quickest way to this bit here?' he pointed to a void beyond the mountainscape.

Possils face fell.

'This is where you want to go?'

'Obviously,' said Lon.

'Well…the quickest way to the Dead Space is through the mountains along the Silent Path.'

Anji tutted. 'Why do all these places have to have such ominous names? Why can't it be called Fluffy Field or something like that?'

Jake laughed.

'The names aren't meant to intimidate, Miss, it's just that no-one goes to these places anymore.'

'Why not?' asked Random.

'Well, they are not quite forbidden as it were, it's just…'

'People went there and never came back, did they?' said Random in a grave tone.

'Typical,' muttered Jake. He rolled his eyes at Anji.

'Never a dull minute,' she tutted back and then shot a sneaky smile at him.

'Well, I suppose we'd better just keep out wits about us,' said Random as he got up off his haunches. 'How safe can we expect to be?'

'Oh you should be fine. Spectron…well, Spectronia to you all, as you know by now is a peaceful planet,' said Possil.

'We should split into two teams. One goes along the open plain, the other through the mountain side. That way we increase our chances of catching up with Strakonis before he moves on…if he moves on,' said Lon.

'You mean, this could be a trap?' asked Random.

'You never know with him,' said Lon. 'Random, if you and your crew are still willing to come we can take both paths. Are you with us?'

Despite the danger and lack of awareness of Lon's overall plan, Random had no hesitation to throw his hat in the ring. Even Anji and Jake, despite their recent urge for a more quiet life, were both thinking that this adventure could be fun. They had caught Random's infectious quest for excitement yet again.

'I'll explain the plan again to Auger and Etherton in a moment. Auger can take your friends Jake and Skateboard through the open plain. The rest of us will take the rocky mountainside, up the Silent Path,' said Lon.

'Oh great, I get the one with the creepy name,' said Anji sarcastically.

'How will we stay in contact?' asked Anji.

'Ah!' Random's spontaneous response made them all jump. He pointed at his two human friends.

'You two, have you got your mobile phones on you?'

Anji felt for the front pocket in her dungarees and produced her handheld device.

'Check!' Jake riffled through his pockets, producing all manner of fluff and rubbish before digging out his.

'Double check!'

'We can modify them so we can stay in contact, Skateboard?' asked Random.

'On it, sir.'

Lon approached the Chief Architect. 'We've got all the equipment we need with us in the buggy. I'm presuming our stuff is no longer confiscated?'

'No, you are free beings now,' Possil reassured. 'And I am relieved for it. You're welcome to scan all the maps you like, just please leave the originals here. They have been in my family for generations.'

'You didn't choose your job then?' asked Jake.

'No, I was born into it.' Possil offered his hand to Random. 'Good luck to you all, and stay safe.' Before you go, can I just ask one small favour?'

'What's that?' asked Random.

'Get I get a photo with you all for my kids?'

IX

Without any delay, mainly at Lon's behest, the travellers were on their way again. The buggy continued across the sand dunes, continuing their original journey and after a couple of hours they had reached the foot of the mountainside.

'Right, this is where we leave you,' said Lon.

'Now take care, you three, that's an order,' said Random.

'Yes Dad!' joked Jake.

They picked up their things and jumped out of the buggy. Jake disembarked first, but caught his foot in the strap of his backpack and fell backwards out of the vehicle and into a crumpled heap.

'Don't worry, I'll look after him, good luck, sir' said Skateboard.

'He's going to need it!' said Random.

'Keep in constant contact,' asked Lon, 'And Auger; make sure that you stick to the plan. If you find Strakonis before we do, do what you can to contain him. Watch out for traps too.'

'No one said anything about traps!' said Jake, dusting himself down.

'He's an archaeologist in possession of one of the most prized artefacts in the universe. Believe me; he knows a few things about traps and how to lay them. He knows we are coming…and he isn't going to make it easy for us to take it from him.'

'We will do what we can, not sure what help the boy will be but the robot will be useful,' said Auger.

'Oi! I might surprise you!' said Jake.

'I won't hold my breath,' Auger sighed.

'Goodbye Lon and good luck.' Auger held her middle three fingers in a salute. Lon and Etherton reciprocated.

'See ya later, alligators,' waved Jake.

Auger threw a digital mapping tablet in Jake's arms and produced a compass from her pocket.

'Come on, time isn't on our side.'

Random and Anji watched on as the figures of Auger and Jake, with Skateboard gliding gracefully next to them disappeared into silhouette and off in the far distance.

The sun was baking down on them now and Etherton, a creature who was more used to the shade and darkness looked pensive.

'We'd better get a move on too, Lon. Any more time in this heat and you may have to leave me behind.'

'If we have to then things might just be starting to look up,' sneered Lon.

Etherton looked indignantly at Anji, who gave him a sympathetic pat on the shoulder.

The buggy swiveled and Lon, using the map that Random had Skateboard produce from the original copy, looked for the opening to the mountainside road.

'He's not very nice to people, is he? You'd have thought he'd be a bit kinder to get people on side,' observed Anji.

'I know. I'm surprised they put up with it, if you ask me,' said Random. 'You struggle in mild heat then, Etherton?' he asked, turning his attention to the mole-like creature.

'My race, like the Spectronians, live underground. We aren't used to prolonged periods on the surface.'

'But Lomes are great scavengers, the best even,' said Lon, 'So it's handy to keep Etherton around. Enough about him. Where are you from anyway?'

'Oh you wouldn't have heard of it,' said Anji.

'Try us,' replied Etherton.

'Well, Jake and I are from Earth.'

'Never heard of it myself. What about you, Random?'

'I'd rather not say.'

'Looks like I'm not the only one keeping secrets, eh, Random?' said Lon, scoffing.

'I did suggest as such back in the prison cell, Lon,' said Random in a teasing manner. 'You're not the only one who keeps his cards close to his chest. If I told you where I came from you would probably shiver at the very mention of the planet's name.'

'I doubt it…besides I'm regretting asking more than anything,' he retorted.

Before Random could respond, the buggy was
thrown into chaos. The passengers screamed and
shouted as they were catapulted from the vehicle
and thrown onto the harsh ground. Random fell
first and caught Anji and they rolled together over
and over, spinning and twirling until they hit the
mountain wall. A nearby sound of crunching metal
was audible to all of them as they eventually came
to a stop.

Panting, Random shook his head, trying to throw
his vision back into focus. As he lay flat on his
back, aching and hurt, he concentrated his gaze on
the sun until there was only one of them and not
the seven or eight he saw immediately after coming
round.

As soon as they all bled together, he struggled to
his feet.

'Anj – are you okay?'

She grunted, face down in the dirt.

'I'll live, what happened?'

He held out his hand and helped her upright.

'Take it easy, sit on that rock over there and catch
your breath,' he helped her onto the boulder and
went over to the others.

Etherton and Lon had fallen not far from them,
but looked like they had come off worse.

'Ah, my arm,' cried Etherton.

'Let me take a look.' Random had limited knowledge when it came to medical situations, but he had skim read first aid during his short stay on Earth. When he caught a sight of Etherton's appendage, he tried his best not to wretch.

It didn't look good. The bone was jutting out at an awkward angle. Random held Etherton's arm gently, the bristles of his hairy arms rubbing against his coarse hands.

'Lon?'

'Yeah, don't worry about me, I'm fine,' said Lon with more than a hint of sarcasm in his voice.

'Then come and help me!'

Lon slowly got to his feet and made his way over to his companion.

'Looks like a nasty break. We need to find the first aid box.'

'First,' cried Etherton, 'Second, third, as many aids as you can find!'

'I'd better call Jake and Skateboard,' said Anji. She got her phone out of her pocket. The screen was smashed.

'Urgh!' she cried, throwing it to the ground in frustration. 'Just my luck!'

'Keep it on you,' said Random. 'They can still contact us if they need to.'

'Yeah, right,' Anji moaned.

Back home she couldn't keep off her phone. Until Random turned up, that was.

Since then she's been so busy saving worlds with her new friends, and the fact that there was no signal in space, or so she thought, using it couldn't have been further from her mind.

But now it had been tinkered with by Skateboard, maybe she could have contacted friends at home if needed. Now it was broken, the glimmer of contact with home was gone. Until she could nick Jakes that was, although the chances of him not smashing it up too were remote as he was often far more careless than she was!

Plus who would pay the phone tariff for a phone call to Earth from thousands of millions of miles away?

Lon finished tending to Etherton, got to his feet and made his way over to what now was little more than a ruined pile of twisted metal. Most of the supplies and equipment had been tipped out and lay strewn across the path. Lon surveyed the wreckage and sighed. Most of their stuff was either on fire or broken.

'We may have to improvise,' he said back to Random. Taking his jacket off, he fashioned it into a sling and knelt down beside the stricken Etherton. Carefully, he and Random took the broken limb and fed it through the sling as Etherton swore in a number of languages that Random has never heard before but one day would endeavour to use himself.

'There,' said Lon as he tied a knot in the back of the jacket.

'Anj, go and take a look in the wreckage, see if you can find the first aid kit,' said Random.

'Why, what are you going to do?' she enquired.

'Find out what caused the accident.'

Random and Lon made their way back to the spot where the crash took place when suddenly they walked into something hard that whacked into their shins.

'What the-' said Lon as he rubbed his lower legs.

Random held his arms out in place. Hesitantly, he felt for the anomaly. Although the area looked as normal as a rainbow road at the foot of a rainbow coloured mountain could do, something felt weird. Using his hands to test their roadblock he discovered what had catapulted the buggy into the air.

'Lon,' he said. 'Your Strakonis friend has a wicked mind. Look.'

He pulled Lon to the side. From their new perspective, there appeared to be a three foot tall roadblock standing in the middle of the road.

'Camouflage,' spat Lon. 'Strakonis is far from a friend. He wants us dead.'

Random nodded.

'We'd better tread more carefully.'

'Random.'

Anji walked towards them, carrying a battered little box with its lid dented outward, full of what looked like pills.

'They will help to numb the pain, confirmed Lon. 'Good. There could be more traps nearby. We can't stay here.'

'You can't be serious?' Random was becoming flabbergasted by his lack of care for the wounded Etherton.

'If we stay here we are leaving ourselves open to more attacks. Take what you can; we're going to have to continue the journey on foot.'

Random shot a look of pure frustration at Anji.

'We'd better do what he says, otherwise he may leave all three of us behind!' he snorted.

'Well, let's hope that Jake and Skateboard are having a better time than us!' said Anji.

*

Jake was through with walking. Auger was much faster, and taller, than he was, and seemed to be taking giant strides ahead of the rest of them.

'Any chance we can go a little slower?' he huffed.

'No.'

He despaired.

'Skateboard, any chance I can get on your back and you can take give me a lift?'

'Negative for now, sir. The extra weight would compound my circuitry and I would have to dedicate more run time to my gravitational elements to maintain a steady pace.'

Although Skateboard knew this information was true, he hoped he hadn't made it too obvious that what he really thought was that Jake needed to improve his fitness.

'Well, we can take our time, I'm sure,' he said in a reassuring way.

'We can't,' said Auger. 'We must get to the rendezvous before nightfall. The temperature on Spectronia decreases significantly in the evening.'

'I'd rather freeze than drown in my own sweat!' Jake cried.

Auger did not possess the longest of fuses when it came to her temper and Jake was trying it thoroughly. 'Is there anything you do except complain?' she said, the spark threatening to light the fuse.

'Lady, I'm a teenager. Trust me, if it was an Olympic sport I'd have the gold, silver AND bronze medals!'

'You say the weirdest things,' she muttered. However, Auger was curious enough to indulge in her annoying counterpart. 'What's a teenager?'

'You don't have teenagers where you come from?'

'Well I wouldn't be asking you if we did, would I?'

Jake frowned. There was no need to bite at him all the time. He began to wonder whether they had been unfortunate enough to find the three grumpiest explorers in the cosmos. Then he remembered. They were on a mission to regain what they felt was rightfully theirs. Of course they were going to be angry. He decided fighting back wasn't the best response.

'Well…it's the age you are at when you go from being a boy or girl into a man or woman.'

'Ah,' she smiled. 'So that explains why you and your friends are so small.'

'Small? On a good day I'm five foot one!'

Auger turned and gave Jake a little smile.

'Does your species not go through the same?' Jake probed.

'No, no we are lumed.'

'Lumed?'

'A fascinating form of gestation,' Skateboard interrupted.

Jake nodded his head as if to acknowledge he was completely in the knowhow of what the word "gestation" meant.

'My people do not reproduce in the conventional way that others do in the universe.'

'How then?' said Jake. 'Do they hatch?'

'No,' replied Auger. She leant closer to the blonde adolescent.

'We're grown. The Kataowa are grown in lumes and batches of 12.'

'I bet its hell remembering everyone's birthdays then!'

'Of course not. We are all born on the same day.'

'Oh,' said Jake. 'Alright Christmas then!'

'Again, you'll have to explain that one to me,' she said.

'Maybe some other time. That's awesome! So you are born fully grown adults?'

'Yes,' she took a glance down at the map, trying to maintain their pace.

'Why twelve? Six boys and six girls?'

'We are neither.'

'What neither boys nor girls?'

'No.'

'But, you look like a woman?'

'I look how I look,' she said firmly.

'There is no need for gender identity on Kataowa, sir,' said Skateboard, 'they do not reproduce like humans, remember?'

'Humans?' Auger cried. 'I thought I heard earlier that you were human. Etherton ran the medical diagnostics after you crashed but I had no idea. Especially after your friend Random's read out nearly broke the computer! So you're from Earth then?'

Jake's jaw dropped. 'How do you know about Earth!?'

'We've been there.'

'What?!' Jake was flummoxed. 'How? When? So the movies were true!?' He was truly astonished that aliens had been to his planet.'

'Centuries ago. Long before your time.'

Jake turned to Skateboard for confirmation that he wasn't going mad.

'Centuries? But you look so young!'

'We don't age. We can live for a long time.'

'It is true, sir, the Kataowa's average life span is just short of two thousand years.'

'So…how old are you now?'

'Don't ask a woman such questions,' she quipped

Jake smiled back at her. Finally he felt like she was starting to warm to him which was something of a blessed relief.

Jake scratched his head. 'I have so many questions right now.'

'Well, which ones the most pertinent?'

'Why did you go there?'

'We were looking for an artefact in a barren desert, not as colourful as this one…boring place, really. Unfortunately for us we had to make a hasty exit. You see, the thing we came for was on a monument and we had to be quick in our escape.'

'What was it you took?'

'An element that we had detected as one of a kind.'

'Yeah?' Jake was eager to know more.

'I won't bore you with the details but your people
had built it into a monument and we took it under
the cover of darkness. Bit of a fiddly one so we
didn't do a good job but I'm sure they fixed it after
we had gone. Knowing how stupid they were, they
probably thought their gods had done something
to punish them or something.'

'Wow. What was it that you actually took?'

'The nose.'

Jake frowned.

'Sounds familiar.' His brain did cartwheels.
Wasn't this something he had learnt at school? Or
was it something he missed whilst daydreaming
out of the history class window? 'Nope, nothing.
Oh well.'

Skateboard searched his memory databases.

'I don't suppose you came across the Osirans
when you were there, did you?'

Auger looked down at the robot.

'They are long gone.'

I wouldn't be too sure of that, he thought.

'Ssshh!' Jake hissed. The group stopped in their
tracks.

'Can you hear that?'

Silence.

'No.'

Skateboard turned up his audio sensors.

'There's something coming from just over that
ridge,' he confirmed.

Auger craned her neck to get a better look.

A huge dust cloud began to fold over the horizon.

'Run,' she muttered.

'What is it?' asked Jake.

'It's a sand storm. Quick, now! Run, run! Get back to the mountain!'

Jake fell to the floor in horror. A burst of brilliant colour exploded into view, crashing over the ridge and looming over them, blocking out the sky.

He scrambled to his feet and shot towards the other two. Ignoring his own wheezy breath and terrible lack of fitness, he pelted as fast as his little legs would carry him. There was a tremendous roar from behind them and a spray of sand particles. Jake began to panic. He reminded himself of the Sandman who blew up their school when they first met Random and the devastation he had caused.

This was like a thousand sandmen put together!

Auger and Skateboard were too quick for him and were tearing away and out of view.

'Wait!' he screamed but he panicked whether they could hear him.

A stitch formed in his side and tears began to collect in the corners of his eyes.

Surely it wasn't going to end like this?

He stumbled forward, his body giving up on him.

Jake didn't have time to curse. He didn't even have time to close his eyes and wait for the inevitable.

This was it.

But then suddenly, something else roared over the sound of the crashing wave.

With a great whoosh of power, Jake was scooped up off his back and the next thing he knew he was gliding through the air, leaving the sand storm far behind.

'Skateboard?'

'Hold on, sir.'

Skateboard zoomed away from danger and into a cavity in the mountainside that Auger had found. They hid behind a small boulder and ducked as the sand storm slammed with such force into the mountain that the world around them shuddered.

Cautiously, Auger looked up over the boulder.

'We'll have to wait here until the storm subsides, great!' she threw a nearby rock into the ground.

Jake held his knees close to his body and tried to regain his breath.

'So much for gravitational dampeners, eh Skateboard?' he rasped. 'But thank you. I thought I was a goner there.'

'It's quite alright, sir, and now you know why I lied the first time around,' he quipped.

X

Unaware of the other group's troubles as they were on the other side of the huge mountainscape, Random continued to fiddle with Anji's phone. Although he was carrying the main bulk of backpacks and equipment, his friend had also insisted on him having a look at her broken device.

'I'm telling you, Anj, even though I am from another world that's more advanced than yours there's nothing I can really do for this,' he gave up after a few minutes of tinkering. 'I left Rodas with a stolen ship and a talking Skateboard, not a computer degree.'

'I thought you'd say that, well, words to that effect. Thanks anyway.' Anji's attention turned to the wounded party. 'How are you coping, Etherton?'

'I've no idea,' he replied. I'm relieved that what Lon lacks in a bedside manner he will make up for in leniency.'

He was holding nothing else but the digital compass as the others carried the weight, with Lon seemingly competing with Random over the amount of cargo he was carrying.

'The pills should reset your arm fully in an hour or two,' reassured Lon.

'Oh good, I'm relieved that you said that. Only two hours of constant agony to endure.'

'Of course, I could always make it go away instantly.'

'Really, how?'

'Let's put it this way, Etherton. If you keep up your moaning I'll put you out of your misery myself!'

Random threw his load down on the floor firmly.

'Lon, if you continue to bully your travelling companions you'll certainly see a less charitable side to me!'

Lon turned. Random was fuming, fists clenched.

'Oh please,' he said wearily. 'You think you can lead this exposition?'

'That's not what I am saying,' said Random. 'But we are volunteers on this expedition and if you keep this abusive stance up we are well within our rights to return to the city and leave you to complete it yourself.'

'I don't want to order you, Random…'

'Good because I wouldn't advise you to try.'

Etherton shook his head. 'Random, please, there really is no need for all this. When you've been with Lon for as long as I have, you learn to ignore his bad moods.'

'That's fine for you to say but we aren't putting up with it,' said Anji.

Lon gave a withering smile.

'Look, this isn't a day trip to the zoo; this is a race against time!'

'We've dealt with worse than this is the past, we'll get over this obstacle, if you stop abusing your workforce. Do we have a deal?'

Lon begrudgingly admired Random for his stance. It takes a lot of courage to stand up to a person like him. But he wasn't the type to apologise.

'Let's keep going,' he replied, before starting off up the path again.

Anji sighed.

'I suppose that's his way of saying sorry!'

'You shouldn't provoke him, Random,' Etherton took his glasses off with one hand and rubbed them against his jacket.

'It's good for him to be reminded that he can't bully his way to winning back this Flux thing,' said Random through gritted teeth.

'Why not? That's how he has got to where he is in life.' Etherton shrugged.

'If it isn't broke, don't fix it, eh?' said Anji.

'Exactly. Lon's a born winner. The Zedron Flux is the first artefact that has ever got away from his grasp. It's also the most important to him. Just take him cautiously.'

'So he isn't always like this?' asked Anji.

'Actually, sadly he is.'

'Hey, come up here!' Lon's voice carried back down the path. The others gathered their things up and raced up to meet him.

Turning the corner, they all noticed why his beckon wasn't a happy one.

'Ah,' said Random.

The path came to a sudden stop. In front of them was nothing but a tower of rock, piled up hundreds of feet into the sky.

'Strakonis again, I presume?' Random said.

Lon nodded. 'According to this map the road should continue through here and continue on for twenty miles.'

'Twenty miles?' Anji and Etherton said in unison.

'Strakonis must have blasted a charge deliberately.' Lon put his map back in his pack.

'Or a rock fall happened by accident?'

'This is no accident,' Lon cursed loudly. 'He's always one step ahead, isn't he?'

'Unfortunately for now we have to play his game to keep up,' said Random, 'but we can turn the tide.'

Lon's eyes narrowed. 'We will. Just makes me mad that I have to dance his merry tune until that eventuality. It's humiliating…but I'll make him pay. Just you see.'

He began to rummage through his backpack.

'Right, there's only one way through and that's over the top.'

'You can't be serious?' said Anji.

'I am never anything but,' said Lon.

'Yes, we noticed that,' muttered Random. 'Fine, let's do it then.'

'But that's going to take forever…and look how high it is! We'll never make it!' Etherton despaired at the thought of climbing. 'Veps are ground beings. Can't I burrow underneath?'

'The rock density will be too great for the tools we have with us, sorry Etherton, on this occasion I can't see any other alternative but go over the top,' said Random.

'What, with my arm like this?'

'I can carry you,' Random smiled.

Etherton's jaw dropped. 'Not with all those bags!'

'Wanna bet?'

'Not really!'

Anji put her hand on Etherton's good arm. 'You'll be fine, Etherton, you'll be in good hands.'

'Oh, so he's taken you piggy backing on a mountain climb before has he?'

'Well…no, but he is incredibly strong.'

'And fast,' Random's eyes were friendly and trustworthy to Etherton. He looked up again and gulped.

'I don't like it.'

'Neither do I but again we are left with no choice,' said Lon as he produced three sets of laser picks. 'That's lucky, there's only three pairs of these anyway. I've got some boot spikes in here too and some bungee cord. Random, you ready to prove just how strong you are?'

'Always,' Random smiled back at him.

'Anj – will you be alright doing this?'

She nodded but deep down her stomach had turned into a butterfly park. On Earth she had climbed a high wall on trips out with the children's home her and Jake lived in and she was fine with that, but comparing this challenge to that was like using chopsticks to cut down a tree. But a spark had lit inside her and a fire was burgeoning for her to be adventurous again.

She'd been heavily affected by her experiences on Genocia, almost hiding from the universe on all those cosmic holiday resorts. But the spirit was awoken within her again.

'Let's do it. But Random?'

'Yes, Anj?'

'If you let me fall to my death I'll kill you.'

She grinned as he laughed.

Random pointed at his friend. 'I'll hold you to that. Right, Etherton, if I tie you to my waste you can ascend up below me along with the bags if you want?'

'Sure, more padding for the inevitable drop!' he replied.

'Good man, right let's get a shake on then.'

He looked up again. The scale of the climb was intimidating but Random hoped that his bravado had done enough to shake off any indication to the others that for him this was going to be much harder, and scarier than he was letting on.

XI

Jake awoke with a startle.

'Sir, sir, Miss Auger has left the cave.'

'She'll be killed!'

'No, I can assure you that the storm has passed. You slept through most of it.'

'Well,' yawned Jake, 'When you've run as much as I just did, it's wise to have a nap to refuel for the next life-threatening dash.'

Wiping his eyes, he got up and shook his head before leaving the cave with Skateboard in tow.

He peered out onto the calm landscape. It was as though nothing had happened. There was no devastation, nothing, just peace and quiet.

Jake scanned the horizon.

'Hey, I thought you said that Auger was out here already?'

'She is…' Skateboard took a look around him. '…At least, she was.'

They both looked at each other.

'Can you scan her? See where she's got to?'

'Doing it now, sir,' said Skateboard. He set his tracking parameters a little wider in distance and surveyed the land.

Nothing.

He widened them further.

Still nothing.

He then switched them to horizontal, thinking
there may be quick sand nearby, in which case, she
was in terrible trouble indeed, and they were
probably too late to help her.

Skateboard switched his sensors with a sense of
dread and learned the terrible truth.

'Sir, I've found her.'

'Great!'

'Not quite, sir. She isn't alone.'

'More tribal warriors? Excellent.'

'No, not that either sir. There's another heartbeat.
A Much, much bigger heartbeat.'

The ground beneath their feet began to shudder.
Jake tried to keep his balance. A rumbling emitted
from under the sand.

Suddenly, a huge creature that looked like a giant
snake, exploded from under them, knocking both
to the floor. It kept going, raising higher and higher
towards the sky, its brown and red body massive
in diameter and wider than a skyscraper.

'Oh my god!' exclaimed Jake.

'Quick get back to the cave!' screamed Skateboard
but before they could move, the creature's vacant,
worm-like head reared down towards them. From
nowhere, a slit opened and a disgusting salivating
mouth began to drool down upon them. Jake cried
in fear. Skateboard leaked his fuel as it was too late
to do anything other than that now.

With one fell swoop, the monster swooped down
and ate both of them whole.

The monster's belly was warm and squidgy. There was nothing for Auger to grapple on to even attempt to climb out from within its hot, putrid stomach. The gloopy remnants of previous meals lay in horrific piles all around her. She tried again, cringing at the slime oozing down the stomach wall before grunting in defeat as she slipped onto the floor of the monster's gut.

She turned to her bag, searching for some dynamite. If she wasn't able to climb her way out, then she'd have to blow it out. The only other escape route was less desirable than death!

Auger huffed. No dynamite. Only a knife. Fat lot of good that'd do, she thought.

All of a sudden, she heard cries from high above her. Quiet at first, but they were getting louder and louder.

She rolled to one side, covering herself in more of the slime, taking evasive action as Jake and Skateboard crashed into the stomach with her sending volumes of yucky gut juice high into the air and crashing back down upon them. Their bodies bounced up and down for a bit, sloshing the contents of the creature's belly all around.

Jake tried to talk but all he could say was a multitude of noises that were incoherent to even Skateboard, who was doing his best to work out what he was exclaiming. He gave up and checked his diodes.

'Anything broken, sir?'

Jake continued to moan and grunt.

'Miss Auger, I'm so relieved to see you're okay.'

'Okay…OKAY!!?' she raged. 'Look at where we are!'

'Present situation withstanding at least we are all well,' said Skateboard, doing his best to look on the bright side.

Jake coughed and wiped his eyes again. There was a foul smelling yellow liquid that poured down his cheeks.

'I think I'm going to be sick,' he declared. 'Am I where I think we are or am I dead and this is my hell? Cos' either way. I think I'm going to need to change my pants!'

'Stop waffling, we need to figure a way out of here,' said Auger as she offered her hand and picked him up onto his feet. 'Skateboard, can you get us out of here?'

'Indeed I can, Miss. But first we shall have to make good of two things.'

'Like?'

'Yes, I can get you all out of here. But first we need to make sure that the creature's mouth is open. We might also be quicker if we can ride a tidal wave of stomach acid.'

'You mean you want to give this thing indigestion?!' cried Jake.

'Precisely. If we stay here too long we may be digested. I surmise that we are currently standing in the creature's stomach. Next stop, the lower intestine. Who knows how long it will be before we move on to its…'

'Well, I'm not hanging around waiting to find out!' said Auger. 'Let's do it!'

'How?' asked Jake.

'I don't know ask your metal friend, I've never been inside a monster before.'

'What are we surrounded by? Smell the air,' implored Skateboard.

They both did and instantly regretted it.

'Poo!' exclaimed Jake.

'Not yet,' corrected Skateboard. 'Does it smell noxious?'

'I'd say!'

'Then that's the answer. Right, you two jump up and down and keep going until I give the signal. I'll start a small fire…'

'We'll go up in smoke!' said Auger.

'No we won't. As soon as a burst of gas propels us upward, I'll swoop us up and send us on our way. Trust me, you two.'

Jake and Auger gave each other an uncertain smile and did what they were told. Ungodly gurgles surrounded them like belches of the damned.

They all hopped and jumped as hard as they could, the sounds becoming louder and louder.

It didn't take long before the sand creature was beginning to feel the effects of the mayhem erupting within its stomach. From deep within its bowels a rumbling sound began to bubble from underneath their jumping feet.

'Oh my god, I think it's working!' exclaimed Jake. 'Please let this work!'

'Here we go! Now!' said Skateboard, in a tone that made Jake and Auger think he was enjoying himself.

A giant surge of gas blew up from within the monster's stomach and spun its unwilling incumbents around and around like socks in a tumble dryer. Jake and Auger screamed and clawed for something to slow them down as they whirled around and around, faster and faster.

Their bodies rose higher with every passing second.

Skateboard, measuring the power of the whirlwind, waited for the right moment to spring to life. He allowed himself to be whisked around like the others in the smelly gas cloud, getting closer and closer to his friends.

'Grab hold of me,' he urged. Auger did as she was instructed.

He maneuvered himself closer to Jake and the boy grabbed hold of the other side of Skateboard's chase.

'Hold on!'

With a jolt of energy, Skateboard fired his retros. This act would have been fairly innocuous were it not for the flammable gas surrounding them but on this occasion it wasn't a very good idea to light a flame when you're inside the body of a dangerous alien creature. Unless, like him, you had an escape plan.

With an amazing force that nearly ripped Jake's face from his skull, the trio were propelled like a bullet back up the monster's neck, clinging to dear life whilst feeling the flames licking at their shoes. Their velocity carried them further towards their escape. Auger began to lose her grip. Skateboard felt her palm imprint begin to slip so he produced two grapples from within his body and fastened them around his friend's waists.

'We're almost there!' Skateboard yelled as another gurgling roar began to rumble. The explosion had ebbed away and they could feel the worm begin to sway.

Skateboard adjusted their flight trajectory accordingly and whooshed around a junction that was actually the monster's neck. Within moments, they smashed through a glunky mass of putrid matter and slammed hard into what felt like a sandy floor.

Skateboard adjusted his optical settings and released the grapples around Auger and Jake's waists.

Panting, struggling to breathe, they lay chests heaving in a gooey mess. The sand clung to their flesh like a second skin. Coughing up a horrific amount of slime, Jake rolled onto his front and gagged repeatedly.

'Do you want me to hold your hair back?' joked Auger.

Finally, Jake managed to stop retching and wiped his eyes clear, rubbing coarse grains of sand back into them.

'Let's…never…do that…again!'

XII

Random and Anji were nothing but the epitome of concentration as they made their assent up the rock face.

They had made a quick start, setting off after Lon who in keeping with his need for urgency was in a rush to get over as quickly as possible.

'Slow down, man, what are you hurrying for, have you got a date?' Random bantered.

'You know damn well why I am rushing.' Lon muttered.

'Lon, we have to put safety first, slow down.' Random barked.

'Safety first? You know how funny that sounds coming from a boy who is carrying our whole entourage?'

'Hey! I'm doing just fine without any help, thanks!' Anji corrected him. She was. Random was proud of her efforts. He knew her adventurous spirit would be reawakened by their quest. This was the friend he had made back on Earth, not the one who was almost too scared to come out of a spa swimming pool and seek out the wonders of the universe with him.

'How far have we got to go do you reckon Etherton?' said Random, trying to involve his passenger in the conversation.

'I don't know, but I wouldn't turn back now,' gulped Etherton. A stiff breeze enveloped them and it was getting worse the higher they climbed.

The Vep had made a terrible mistake in looking over his shoulder at the ground below. It was a disconcertingly long way away now.

'As long as our magnetic clips and laser picks work we shall be fine,' Lon reassured him. 'I reckon we are at about half way.'

With considerable effort, Random pulled one of his pick axes out of the rock face and smashed it half a foot higher up and repeated the same motion again and again. He had insisted on climbing up last in the off chance that Anji may get into some difficulty. But then, what would he do if she were to fall? He couldn't fly, so grimly, Random had come to the conclusion that he would have to smother her and plummet with his friend in his arms and do his best to break her fall. He knew he was strong and had a metabolism that would make an olympic rower green with envy, but could he survive a fall from such a great height?

Random shook the thought from his head, hoping he would never have to find out.

He felt the strain of his cargo. Clinks and sounds of tortured guide ropes shredded his nerves with every passing foot up the mountain.

'Anj, are you okay?'

'Of course, I'm just doing what you said and not looking down.'

Anji gritted her teeth. Inside she was screaming in terror. One false move and she was dead. No matter how hard she tried to reassure herself, this was the most terrifying thing she had ever done.

She had tried to brush off the climb by comparing it to a high wire event she had taken part in on a school trip. She had struggled to equate walking along a wire bridge suspended ten metres above the ground with a full scale climb up the side of an alien mountain. No matter how much she had tried to convince herself she was back in that adventure fun land, the mirage didn't work.

A cold sweat hung around her face, gluing strands of her hair that had fallen out of her ponytail to her clammy cheeks and forehead. Aware that she was shaking, Anji threw the pick axe into the rock faster and faster, trying her best to keep up with Lon.

Slow and steady was the safer method, yes, but the quicker they got to the top, the faster this ordeal would be over.

Noticing that Anji had picked up the pace, Random scowled.

'Anji! Slow down.'

'I can't Random, I just can't! I've got to get to the top.'

She picked quicker and quicker, her body aching to feel safe again.

'Anj please! Calm...'

Suddenly one of Anji's pick axes failed to imbed itself in the rock and it bounced out of her hand. Losing her grip, she fumbled at thin air with her now free hand and she screamed as her gaze followed the axe down below. She froze, paralysed with fear. Anji could feel her heart beating in her head. Nothing but terror coursed through her blood. She could hear nothing but her short, sharp breaths of fear.

'Zart!' swore Random. He picked up his own pace. Etherton complained as he and the cargo bounced after him, causing more stress on the already tortured guide ropes.

Anji's head began to swim. Her body was frozen but her mind was on the verge of blacking out.

Lon looked back at the commotion below. There was nothing he could do. It would be perilous for him to back up. He had to keep going. If he stopped for too long, who knows, maybe he may freeze up too? Reluctantly, he furrowed on.

'Anj, hold on, I'm nearly there!' cried Random.

Tears trickled out of the corners of her eyes.

She tried to speak but could not easily.

'I-I-I don't think I can…' she croaked.

'Just a few more seconds, please!'

She planted her forehead against the colourful rock face. It felt smooth, cold against her sweaty skin.

A small twang emitted from one of the cargo bags Random was hauling.

Etherton's face turned white as he noticed what was starting to happen.

'Random…the weight, we can't take it!' he pleaded.

At that moment, everything was thrown into chaos.

Panic and terror overwhelmed Anji and she lost consciousness and her hands slipped off the axe and she began to fall backwards.

'No!' yelled Random as he swung upward. As he leapt up the rock face, the guide rope tore in two, sending the cargo and Etherton tumbling towards the earth. The mole-like man managed to hang on with his harness and catch one of two of the bags before they tumbled back down the cliff face, but the bounce from the displacement of weight unbalanced Random. Stretching every sinew in his arm, he just managed to prop Anji up. Her boots were still implanted in the rock, but now that her weight was facing downward, they wouldn't stop her fall for long.

'Lon!' he hollered, but the explorer was too far away to help. Surely he had heard the commotion?

Random grunted as he tried to pull Anji away from the wall as Etherton continued to whimper below him. He dare not look down to see how he was getting on.

'Etherton, are you okay?' strained Random.

'No!' cried Etherton. 'There's too much weight. We're going to fall!'

'We are not going to fall!' cried Random. He tried to search his mind. His grip on the pick axe was starting to get awfully sweaty.

'Is there anything in those bags we can expend?'

Etherton struggled to find an answer.

'Um…in theory the tool bag.'

'Then drop it.'

'But without it we won't be able to pick up the Flux! The containment field is in there.'

'Just do it! I can't hold onto you all forever!'

Etherton hesitated. Then he remembered their predicament. Rather a bag of heavy tools than his own sorry skin. Scrunching his eyes tight, he let go of the bag.

Random levered himself upward and scooped Anji up fully with his arm. He held her tight to his side.

'Right, let's get moving again before anything else falls off!'

Etherton poked him in the back.

'Just one thing, Random. How are we going to climb if you've only got one free hand?'

Random went blank.

'Ah…'

'Random!'

They looked up. The voice in the distance was Lon's.

'Grab hold of this!'

From afar, what looked like a thin metal ladder descended from the top of the cliff face.

Random sighed with relief.

He watched as the ladder tumbled further and further towards them and then it stopped abruptly roughly ten feet away from them.

'Lon, it's too short, bring it closer!'

'I can't,' came the distant voice.

Random searched his thoughts for an idea. All of a sudden, one popped into his head. A very silly one.

'Etherton, you're going to have to hold on for dear life.'

'As if I'm not already!'

'I'm going to have to jump for it. Hold on to my leg.'

Etherton's jaw dropped.

'We'll never make it!'

'Yes we will, trust me!'

'No!'

'Okay then, humour me.'

Etherton did what he was told and clasped his paws around Random's leg.

'One.'

'No.'

'Two.'

'No!!'

With a fantastic leap, Random propelled himself, the unconscious Anji and a screaming Etherton upwards, away from the pick axes. He had to make it. If he had miscalculated his own spring, then they wouldn't be getting any higher anytime soon!

The whole world seemed to fall silent around them. It was like they were moving in slow motion.

With an outstretched arm, Random gratefully clasped his grip round the bottom rung of the ladder and gave an almighty sigh.

'We did it! We did it!' cried Etherton. 'I always knew you would.'

Random gave his companion a withering look.

'We made it! Right, winch us up!'

'No can do, I'm afraid,' replied Lon. 'The ladder is fastened down. I'm afraid you'll have to climb up.'

Random clicked his tongue.

'Fine, be with you in a minute.'

He turned to Etherton and smiled.

'There, you can let go now, how's that arm holding up?'

'You know what? A perilous situation seems to wonders for blanking out pain!' he said as the ache began to return when he noticed that it was his broken arm that was hanging onto Random's leg.

'Not to worry, about another hundred metres and we will be safe. Let's get going. We need to get Anji to safety.'

'Yes, and us!' Etherton reminded him.

Random used the arm carrying Anji to throw her over his shoulder. Wedging her legs in under his arm, he grunted as he began to climb again.

Slowly, they began their assent back up the rock face.

Random did well to maintain his balance on the climb. Throwing Anji over one shoulder had given him better stability on the ladder, but knowing full well what danger he had exposed his friend to, he began to curse this whole experience.

Oh Anji, he thought to himself, *I hope you will forgive me or putting you through this…*

A world of familiar voices whirled around Anji's head. They bounced to and fro around the blackness inside her mind. Slowly, she started to open her eyes and quickly wish she hadn't. The piercing light of the Spectronian sun swarmed her. The recent memory of the terrifying plummet far below her didn't. She let them roll back into her head and slumped back onto what felt like solid rock.

And then, she remembered.

She'd blacked out on the cliff face.

But how was she still alive? Surely she should have fallen to her death? Unless the ground beneath them was made of some sort of quilted material, she should be by all rights dead.

'Anj!' cried a relieved Random. 'Are you okay?'

She kept her eyes shut.

'I take it this isn't heaven then?'

'What makes you say that?'

'You're here.'

Random smiled. 'Oh, Anji Gummadi is back alright!'

She tried to get up but her head was still swimming.

'Just sit there for a bit. You've had a nasty shock.'

'What happened?'

'I asked too much of you. Anji, I'm so sorry, I'll never put you through anything like that again.'

'Too bloody right you're not!' she jabbed his arm. 'Are we back on the ground?'

'No, we kept on going. Lon was able to bail us out of trouble. Anj, we're at the top of the cliff face and the others have discovered something which might help us get to Strakonis much quicker than we thought.'

'A short cut?' asked Anji.

'You bet,' said Lon. 'We've found a cave opening. Etherton is checking the route out now for bugs and traps. How's it going, Etherton?'

Etherton had placed himself on a small rock and was watching a tiny monitor with great intent.

'The probe has covered roughly four miles of tunnels, so that's the Silent Path, and there's no sign of any obstruction so far. I estimate it's got about another mile to go before it reaches the ground…ah! There it is!'

Lon rushed to his aide's side. He pressed his face into the monitor.

A brilliant green shone through the screen.

'The Flux! But it can't be.'

Random got up and joined them.

'So that's what's causing all of this danger.'

'Isn't it worth it?' said Lon, with a look that was close to love in his eyes.

'It's very beautiful, I have to confess,' Random confirmed. 'It's a bit close. Too unguarded, I don't like it. I thought we had much more of a journey on our hands than just in the centre of a mountain?'

'Well, we all did…but look!' Etherton's finger pointed at a figure moving in the shadows.

Lon's eyes narrowed.

'Strakonis…'

'What's he doing there?' asked Etherton.

The trio watched on as the shadow busied himself in what looked like a narrow cavern. It appeared that he was fixing what looked like charges into the rock walls.

'Setting booby traps for us,' said Lon.

'He doesn't want us to get out of this alive by the looks of it,' said Random. 'Those charges are thermo detonators. As soon as a living being comes into range, boom!'

'He'll do anything to keep the Flux from my grasp,' Lon made for his bags and rummaged hastily. 'Well, I say it's time that we fought fire with fire!'

He produced a small laser gun from his bag.

'Not on my watch,' said Random sincerely.

'Look Random, you've seen he means to kill us.'

'It doesn't mean he will. Besides, we know what he has planned for us now.'

'Lon…surely you wouldn't?' Etherton had known Lon for a long time. He'd known his ambition to outstretch his capability to hold it together before but never had he witnessed his old colleague so driven as to even think about killing a rival.

'That man has taken the most powerful energy source in the cosmos. Think of what the Flux can do in the wrong hands!'

Random was silent.

'I suggest we proceed with caution. Nothing more.'

Lon cussed as he pocketed his weapon.

'Okay, Random, we will play it your way…for now.'

'No killing, Lon!'

'I'm not a killer, Random!'

'Not yet…'

Lon walked right up to Random, pressing his face into his own. Random did not flinch.

'Who the hell do you think you are?'

'I'll tell you. I'm someone who has seen madness and evil walk hand in hand. Make sure you don't join the two and we'll continue to get on.

But if this Strakonis fella tips you too close to the edge, you bet that I'll be the one pulling you back before you do something stupid.'

Lon's face was a picture of pure frustration, desperation even. Anji got to her feet and was speechless.

She knew Random could handle him, but the longer they spent with Lon, the more dangerous he became.

'Cool it, you two,' said Etherton, trying to squeeze between them.

Lon shot daggers at Random. 'We should have left you back in your ship...'

His words chilled Anji. If they hadn't of rescued them, they'd have been dead for sure.

Random just stood there, staring, unblinking, unnerved.

Lon moved away, staring with deadly intent at Random until he pulled his back pack up towards him and fastened himself defiantly. 'Etherton.'

Etherton gulped and wiped his forehead.

'Coming.'

Random stayed exactly where he was standing. As Lon and Etherton moved off towards the cave mouth, Anji approached her friend.

'We can't go back.'

'I know.'

'So why do you keep provoking him? You're making an enemy of Lon.'

'He's making an enemy of himself,' Random watched as they disappeared around the corner.

'Besides, we've seen his kind before. Corrupted by greed, a lust for power. Sound familiar?'

'All too much,' Anji shuddered. The experience of Genocia was going to be a memory that would live long with her.

'If this Flux thing is as powerful as they have been saying it is, then think of the untold devastation it can cause.'

'In the wrong hands…' said Anji, allowing the sentence to run away from her. 'So that's why we couldn't leave them. That's why we had to come along.'

Random nodded.

'We have to make sure the Flux ends up in the right hands. The universe may be depending on us.'

'Bit of a grand statement that,' Anji sniggered.

'I'm serious.'

Her smile evaporated.

'I know. Come on then. Let's go save the universe.'

Random wanted to smile, he really did, but the implications of their mission were weighing heavy. Anji was worried. Random seemed troubled.

'You okay?'

'Yes,' he lied. 'Come on.'

Random made for the cave mouth fast with Anji in tow.

She couldn't help but wonder what was wrong with him.

Sure, the Flux was a dangerous component, but they've dealt with less in the past than this. Hadn't they?

Random gritted his teeth.

'Not now. Please, not now,' he whispered to himself.

The voices were back.

XIII

It was getting late. Darkness was casting a shadow over the skies high above the weary explorers. On an alien planet, even one as beautiful and unimposing as Spectronia, to be stuck in the desert at night time is not the wisest of moves. Especially when you have spent a portion of the day trapped inside the intestinal tract of an alien sand monster.

Jake had felt like they had been trekking through the desert for hours. When he stated this as an observation, Skateboard said nothing but silently confirmed to himself that they had indeed been going for a very long time.

He had also stated, much to the boy's dismay that having carried them both for such a long time after what would later be referred to as, "the stomach upset incident" that his energy cells were starting to drain.

He insisted they get off and walk beside him while he scanned for shelter so he could reserve his battery.

'As if you run off a battery,' frowned Jake.

'Doesn't all life in the universe?' said Skateboard smarmily. 'Sorry, sir, but as you can tell I am rather tired. I spend such sufficient time on board the Venus II that I can absorb the power from the ship whenever I start to run low.

But I've never been outside for so long and I could do with switching off soon to preserve my run time. I'll scan the local area for somewhere for us to recharge.'

Jake looked up. The sky was a brilliant wash of mauve light blending in with the darkness. Stars began to twinkle like tiny pearls, shining brighter than any blanket of stars Jake has ever seen before.

'Wow,' he mouthed. 'I can think of worse places to be stuck. What do you think, Auger?'

Auger was very quiet. She had barely said a word since their escape and it unnerved Jake. In their brief time together, he had come to accept that she wasn't the most talkative of people. But his travelling companion had been as silent as a shadow for too long to ignore it as a character trait.

'What's eating you?' said Jake.

Auger gave him a cold look.

'Are you serious?'

'Sorry, poor choice of words,' he replied, reminding himself of their ordeal by catching a whiff of his clothes in the dusky breeze.

Auger soldiered on. 'We should keep going.'

'Surely you can't be serious?' said Skateboard.

'Auger, we've already been eaten today. Who knows what else could be out here!'

'If we don't keep going we are giving Strakonis a chance to escape. We can't let that happen.'

'I understand your frustration, Miss Auger, but if we don't stop we might not get there at all.'

Skateboard completed his scans. 'There's a small hut roughly 500 metres due west. We can set up camp there for the night.'

'But we've only got ten miles left to go! We'd be there in a few hours!'

'Woman, I'm pooped,' said Jake. 'I'm siding with Skateboard.'

'Then I am going on alone!'

'I'm afraid that would be unwise,' advised Skateboard.

'Oh yeah, right, because you two are so powerful to stop me. The boy and the toy.'

'Hey, I'm 13!' said an indignant Jake.

'I don't care, I am not stopping!'

Skateboard sighed. 'Miss Auger, I beg you to think rationally for a moment. Strakonis could have guards, an army even, we don't know how well protected he is. Safety is greater in numbers.'

'Company slows me down. I would have been there already, probably with the Flux already within my grasp, if it wasn't for you two!' She argued.

'You can't blame us for the sand snake, surely? You were the one who got eaten first!' said Jake.

'Hold your tongue before I cut it out!' Auger produced a knife from her pocket.

'Woah, Auger come on, will you just calm down!'

A small taser shot out of Skateboard's body and was pointed firmly in the direction of the threatening Auger.

'Drop it.'

Auger smiled and uneasy grin. 'Sorry, I'm so sorry.'

Slowly, she put the knife away and Jake's heart rate began to climb down.

'I…that's not me. That's not who I am, I don't know what came over me, sorry.'

'You sure about that?' asked Jake.

Auger looked ashamed. Defeated.

'It won't happen again.'

Skateboard slowly retracted the taser.

'Let's get to the hut.'

Brilliant, he thought to himself. *That's a recharge out of the question.*

Skateboard knew that now he would have to stay up all night and watch Auger like a hawk.

Before long, the group had made it to the hut. Luckily it was uninhabited for the time being, although it looked like someone had been there recently. The place was small but a complete mess. Sand seemed to coat every piece of furniture strewn untidily around the place, although there wasn't much to speak of. A small table and a single chair sat beside a long abandoned fire and a blanket that resembled a welcome mat in its cleanliness.

'Could use a spring clean,' said Jake wearily.

'I concur,' Skateboard agreed, although keeping
to himself that it was cleaner than Jake's own
quarters back on the Venus II. 'If we camp here for
the night, we should all feel better for the final leg
of the journey and we will be there before we know
it. Do we have a deal, Auger?'

Auger nodded silently.

Jake dropped his bags and stretched his arms
wide, emitting a loud yawn as he did so. 'Right,
let's get some kip then. I think I've got the sleeping
bags on me. Shame I didn't pack a mattress
though!'

It didn't take long for Jake to fall into a deep,
dreamless sleep, which was odd for him, because
normally, he dreamt an awful lot. His favourite
was a recent one he had when he and his friends
had been staying on the health farm planet of
Zlatacosta Meganion.
It involved him being crowned footballer of the
year for the ninth year in a row and being
rewarded with a knighthood from the Queen
before being fed into a canon and shot into the side
of the moon.

Although it had seemed very real and vivid, and
at the end pretty weird and scary, he'd thoroughly
enjoyed it, apart from the end bit…but it did put
into question whether he was eating too much
cheese before he went to bed.

Skateboard was doing his best to fight back fatigue but his charge was now on 1%. He'd have to switch off soon. But Auger, he couldn't trust her, not after the last episode.

She herself hadn't slept a wink. As she lay on her side, back turned on her counterparts, she could sense that Skateboard had his eyes trained on her. *Pretty remarkable for a robot without eyes*, she thought, *but even he won't see what's coming his way.*

After much soul searching, talking herself in and out of it multiple times overnight, she settled on the horrendous conclusion that she had no choice but to do it. Lon would never forgive her if she didn't put the Flux first. Their wealth depended on her.

Suddenly, Auger stirred and got up, snaked her sleeping bag down her body and walked over to Skateboard.

'Miss Auger. Are you having trouble sleeping?'

'Yes.'

'Is there anything I can do to help?'

'I'm sorry, Skateboard.'

Skateboard whirred. 'It's alright, Miss Auger, I understand the frustration you must be feeling.'

'No, I mean I'm really very sorry.'

Auger plunged her dagger deep into Skateboard's body, hitting his energy pack.

A short scream from the AI robot bleated through the still night as blue lightning-like energy seeped out of the wound, the sound of pierced metal ringing in Auger's ears.

She pushed the blade deeper until nothing but a low sigh emitted from the stricken robot.

Auger withdrew her weapon.

The cabin fell silent again.

Skateboard was dead.

Jake stirred from within his sleeping bag.

Auger flipped backwards and stood up over him.

'Skateboard?' the boy cried as his face peaked out from within the bag's opening.

With one cruel, swift swipe of her boot, Auger kicked Jake full on in the face and knocked him out cold. She proceeded to stuff him back into his sleeping bag and using the cord, fastened the unconscious boy inside like he was being forced deeper into a dark cocoon.

Auger picked it up and swung Jake over her shoulder with minimal effort and picked up the lifeless Skateboard.

'Sweet dreams, you two.'

XIV

'You must go home.'
'Why won't you face your destiny?'
'How will Rodas survive?'
'How will the people survive?'
'Evil must not conquer.'

The voices continued…relentlessly plaguing Random's mind.

'Random…Random…Random…'

'Random?'

The purple boy turned to face his friend. His face was illuminated by the natural fluorescent light on the walls, washing the pair in a spectrum where any other cave system in the universe they would have been submerged in pitch black. Even through the colours, Anji could tell that something was wrong by the expression on Random's face.

'What's up?'

'Nothing,' Random lied. His face was caked in tiny beads of sweat. 'Hot down here, isn't it?'

'Far from it!' said Anji. She took her friends' arm. He felt hot to the touch. 'You know you can tell me if anything is the matter, don't you?'

Random smiled. 'Of course.'

He hesitated.

'Anj – I'm-'

Suddenly, they heard an explosion further on in the cave.

'Lon!' cried Anji.

'Quick!'

Random and Anji tore towards danger, something they seemed to have done a lot ever since they first met. Soon they came to a cloud of rainbow dust. Anji held her sleeve up over her mouth. Random just coughed his way through.

'Lon!' Random spluttered.

'Yes, we're fine,' said a voice that sounded Lon.

As the dust settled, Anji spotted Etherton lying underneath a small pile of rubble.

'Well, speak for yourself!' he remarked. Anji and Random helped pull him clear as Etherton complained about them tweaking his still healing arm.

'Anything broken…again?' asked Random.

'Only my pride this time. We walked straight into a thermo mine. Luckily it didn't get us.'

'Lon, where are you?'

'Right here,' said Lon. He was concealed past the rubble. 'Blasted scout probe didn't pick up one of the mines. Had it not have been for my quick reactions we'd have both been killed.'

'You could have warned me!' complained Etherton.

'You're alive, aren't you? Now if you are quite finished moaning we need to keep going.' Anji huffed at Lon as he displayed yet more of his superb empathy.

'Hold it, what if the cave is now unstable?' Random pointed out.

'What if it isn't?' frowned Lon.

'You want to risk it?'

'I am willing to risk anything for the Flux, even you,' he sneered.

'Well, that's not very friendly, what have we said about your manners, Lon?' scoffed Random. 'And if that's supposed to shut me up then I'm afraid you've got me all wrong.'

Lon smirked. 'No, it wasn't, but this will.'

Suddenly, the suspicious explorer sprayed some sort of gas from a tiny can concealed within a compartment in his waistcoat. Before he had a chance to respond, Random was hit full on in the face with the noxious gas. His head began to swirl and before long, he found himself falling against the wall and slipping to the ground.

'Random!' Anji dropped Etherton to the floor and raced over to her friend. 'What have you done to him?'

'Knocked him out of course, what else do you think I've done? Etherton, grab her!'

Anji acted fast and evaded the mole-like creature's grasp and launched herself at Lon. She pushed him to the floor and attacked him viciously, lashing out with her fists and her palms, smacking him repeatedly, tears forming in her eyes as the anger and fear inside her boiled into a bitter counter attack.

Etherton watched nervously as they grappled but Lon's superior strength soon told as he picked her up and threw her against the wall, completely knocking the wind out of her sails. Anji cried out in pain as he fell to the ground, curling up in a ball and coughing violently.

'Tie her up, now!' he demanded, wiping blood from his lip. His face was scratched, aching from the girl's violent actions.

'With what?'

'With rope, you idiot! Do it or I'll break your other arm!'

Etherton made for a bag and began to rummage around.

'Lon…this is wrong, what are you doing?'

'Taking back the power,' he hissed. He drew a gun and levelled it at Random and Anji's prostrate bodies.

'I have an idea for where we can put them…somewhere they will never be found…'

*

Jake awoke with a startle, not to mention an angry headache.

His jaw ached badly. He groaned softly and moved his hand to cradle it.

Only he couldn't.

He tried again, still no luck.

His hands were bound behind his back.

Jake's surroundings were dark, ominous.

Soon, he realised where he was.

He was in his sleeping bag. The opening had been fastened above his head. But why was he tied up?

Then he remembered.

'Auger! Let me out! Come on, jokes over. Very funny. I'm used to pranks like this. Granted I've never been physically assaulted at the same time, that's a new one…'

Shut up, he told himself. *Stop trying to be funny. This isn't the time.*

'Skateboard?'

He listened for a response. None was forthcoming.

He smelt the air. There was an earthy aroma surrounding him. He tried to wiggle himself free, but he was barely able to move.

Where was he?

Jake tried to wrestle his hands out of his bonds but to no avail.

He did his best to ignore the pain in his jaw but it was hard to do such a thing when it persisted to throb uncontrollably.

Then, with a terrible moment of realisation, he thought he knew where he was.

He was in the ground.

Surely not?

'Please, god no!' he pleaded as he tried to kick himself free.

But it was true. He was lying in a shallow grave.

'Auger! Auger! For god's sake let me out please!'

Soon he began to hyperventilate.

Through gritted teeth he tried to force his hands through the bonds, but it felt like they were plastic, incapable of breaking.

Jake tried to calm his breathing before he was sick. He hated confined spaces. He didn't like to mention it, especially when he was trying to be as brave as Anji and Random. He had a fear of looking weak in front of his friends. Jake had hoped and prayed a tight situation such as this might never come up.

He tried to think clearly, come up with an escape plan.

A vision of a mobile phone came into his head. 'My phone!'

Of course, he thought, *I can call Anji for help.*

Desperately, Jake tried to pull his jacket pocket over. He knew it was there, he could feel it pressing against his stomach.

Auger hadn't removed it. *Stupid…whatever she was again.*

Thankfully, he managed to reach it. Knowing his pin number off by heart, the muscle memory of entering it many times meant even with his hands tied Jake had no problem in remembering the layout and to his relief he opened it up.

The screen illuminated his makeshift coffin. He wished it hadn't.

The light all but confirmed that he was indeed buried under the sand. Grains were starting to trickle in the slight crack in the sleeping bag opening the more he wriggled and the more the opening stretched.

Welling up, Jake tried to remember where his contacts were stored on his phone. It'd be easy to find Anji's number in his call history. She was the only person he ever phoned and the only person who ever wanted to get in contact with him back on Earth.

*

Dangling high above a perilous drop, Anji awoke with a startle. Her surprise escalated to sheer terror when she saw that she had been suspended by a rope around her waist above a cavernous, bottomless pit. She tried to scream, then discovered her vocal chords were too shredded with fright to emit any sound.

The more she moved the more she spun around, hands tied in front of her under the rope around her midriff, she noticed, much to her relief, that she was not alone.

'Random! Random wake up!' she demanded but it was no use.

The Rodasian was still unconscious.

Whatever Lon had sprayed in his face must have been strong to keep even someone as strong as Random asleep for quite a while. She felt a tiny bruise on the back of her head and hoped that she had given Lon more than that before he captured her!

Anji's desperate eyes scanned Random's features. He appeared to be gritting his teeth, as though he were applying a great deal of force.

His eyes were screwed shut so tightly that tiny tears were collecting on his eyelashes.

She tried to maneuver her hands upwards to check his pulse but then she remembered he was an alien. It could be sky high for all she could know and that would be normal for Random. It wouldn't be amiss for him to have no pulse either!

Something was terribly wrong with Random, and that in some ways scared Anji more than the drop.

She sighed and her head fell against her chest. Powerless, she just hung there, limp, helpless.

Silence in the mountain. Lon and Etherton were long gone.

They had failed.

All of a sudden, a familiar ring tone echoed around the cavern. Anji's eyes lit up.

'Oh my god!'

Anji fumbled her bonded hands into the front pocket of her dungarees.

The screen was still as broken as it had been, but somehow, miraculously, it was still receiving calls.

She pressed the fractured screen to accept the call and tapped again to put the caller on loudspeaker.

'Jake! Your sense of timing couldn't be any better!' she returned it to her pocket and pulled the zip a little so she didn't lose the phone to the abyss.

'Anj...'

Jake sounded upset. Anji didn't like it when he was crying. It was so out of character for him. It scared her almost as much as Random being unresponsive.

'What's the matter, where's Skateboard?' she asked.

'Auger...she's buried me...in the desert.' he sobbed.

'Buried you!?'

Jake sniffed. 'She's tied me up and thrown me in the ground.'

'How? Why? Where's Skateboard?'

'I don't know, he's not here. Anji, you've got to come and find me...the sand...it's getting inside my sleeping bag. I'm scared.'

Anji's eyes welled up. 'So am I. Lon's captured us. Something's up with Random too. He's knocked out next to me and we're dangling above a pit.'

Jake couldn't speak. He allowed the sobs to take him over before snorting them back inside monentarily. Anji began to weep.

Jake sucked his cry inward and bought himself a couple of seconds to speak. 'A right pair we make, eh?'

Anji laughed.

There was a moment's silence between them.

'How did we let ourselves get into this Anj?' asked Jake.

'Random did warn us.' Anji replied.

'I know it's not his fault but…I don't know, I'm so scared right now I can't think straight.'

Anji sniffed. 'Me too.'

'The thing is…it's quite exciting, most of the time, isn't it?' Jake snorted as he spoke.

'Yeah.'

'Not now though.' Jake took a look in the murky gloom. 'Anj, I'm going to die here, aren't I?'

'Don't say that!' she pleaded. 'You're alive, that's all that matters.'

'I'm not sure how much longer I'll be able to breathe…'

Tears began to roll silently down Anji's cheeks.

'Listen, remember that promise we made to each other back at the pond? Before Random crashed right in front of us?'

'Kind of hard to forget, a thing like that,' he scoffed.

'Remember what we said to each other. The promise we kept to ourselves?'

Jake smiled. 'Yeah. If we were both single come prom then we'd go together.'

'Well I'm game if you still are?'

Jake sniffed loudly.

'Something tells me I won't be able to make it now.' He almost sounded like he had been grounded by an angry parent.

What he would give for a parent right now, angry or not, someone else to comfort him, to care him. To miss him.

'Of course you will! Just hang on in there and I'll hang in here…' she cringed at her poor choice of words.

'Shh, Anj.'

Jake craned his ear. His sobs died down as something began to move above him.

'What is it?'

'I must be going mad…I could have sworn I just heard footsteps.'

'Well scream then!' Anji urged.

Jake hollered for help as loud as his lungs would allow. Again and again he yelled, trying hard to not to choke on his own snot, shouting so loud that it was a miracle he didn't rip his vocal chords the volume of his cries.

'For god's sake help me!'

Anji prayed on the other end of the line that their prayers would be answered.

There was a long, long silence.

Anji began to worry.

Had Auger come back to finish off the job? She shuddered.

Suddenly, the sound of a spade plunging into the sand pierced through the airwaves.

'Anj…I'm being rescued! I'm being rescued!'

'Good! Then get your arse to the mountain and get us out of here!'

'As long as the prom date stands, I'll be there faster than you can say, "Should I wear my hair up or down, Jake!"'

Anji laughed. 'Alright mister, just make sure you are safe and get here as soon as you can.'

At that moment, the phone went silent.

'Jake? Jake? Jake!?'

Her phone light was dead.

She waited for him to call back, but the screen stayed black.

She sighed. The call wasn't coming. Her phone must have run out of battery. Unless Auger really had come back to finish the job, she wondered.

No, she couldn't think like that. He was going to be safe, he had to be.

She looked at the void below her dangling legs and wished she was too.

*

The digging became more and more frantic. Copious amounts of sand kept tumbling into the sleeping bag like a dry waterfall, making Jake panic again slightly. Would he drown before he managed to get out? Through his screams he thought he could hear a deep, masculine voice.

'Stop moving, you're making it worse. Nearly there.'

It wasn't a voice that Jake recognised. He wondered if the owner of the hut had returned. If so, how lucky was he!

Another brush with death that he had survived.

He tallied in his mind the scorecard between him and certain doom up until now.

Jake - Three
Death - Nil

Another one for old Jakey boy!

Soon, the digging stopped and a pair of gloved hands delved deep into the bag, clutching Jake's face.

'Oi, get off!' he muffled through what tasted like dirty leather fingering the contours of his tear stained face.

He was soon startled as he was picked up out of the ground with considerable ease. Jake slumped to the bottom of the bag and groaned as his backside made hard contact with the ground.

Suddenly, a large knife split through the bag and tore it apart. It must have been early morning by now as Jake squinted hard as the bright sunshine bore into his barely open eyes.

He whimpered as he felt the cold metal of the knife up against his wrists.

'Hold still.'

Jake obeyed.

Shortly, the stranger had finished sawing through his bonds. Jake clambered towards him, clutching his leg and wrapped his body around it.

'Thank you, oh my god, thank you so much!'

The stranger towered above him, his features protected by a cloth mask that concealed his nose and mouth.

'You should try and find better places to sleep.'

Jake giggled and then remembered.

'My friends…they are in danger too. We've got to help them!'

'One thing at a time.'

Jake clambered to his feet gingerly. He caressed his bruised jaw and winced as he felt the hot, split flesh. Grains of sand had fallen into the cut, aggravating an already angry wound.

'Who are you and what are you doing there?' asked the stranger.

'I'm Jake. I came here with friends but we've been betrayed…oh my god, Skateboard where is he?'

'Betrayed? By who?'

Jake held his hand to his eyes, shielding the sunshine from his gaze.

'First of all, who should I thank for saving my life?'

The stranger unveiled his mask. Jake recoiled instantly. The man's face was badly scared.

'My name is Strakonis.'

XV

Somewhere, deep within his own psyche, a battle was enraging between Random and his sanity. Whilst unconscious, he had been present in a sort of purple void. It looked like some form of tunnel, a literal bypass linking him between his inner thoughts and his own mind. He tried to shake the concept of being inside his own head from his thoughts and began to wonder if he was dead. Perhaps Lon finished him off whilst he was knocked out?

Maybe this was the afterlife. That's a turn up, he thought!

He then groaned audibly as he realised that being gassed was perhaps one of the lamest ways to go he could think of. Why couldn't it be something heroic? He'd been heroic many times of late, anything but a whiff of smelly stuff to put him firmly in the ground.

Seemingly unable to move, he noticed what looked like people up ahead. Two of them, floating angelically.

He called out to them. 'Hey! What am I doing here? Not that I'm sure where here is. I need to get back, my friend is in trouble.'

They did not respond.

Now Random knew he was definitely

unconscious and not pushing up the daisies as he had feared. He had twigged it.

He wasn't really in limbo. But it felt like he was drifting between plains, flitting between life and death. Suddenly, it dawned on him who the two figures were supposed to represent.

'You're…the voices in my head, aren't you?'

They remained silent.

'So that must make you…'

A feeling of shock convulsed through Random's body.

'…no, it can't be!'

He was confused, more confused than he had ever been.

'But…I don't understand. I came out of that big tube thing. You two can't be…'

The ghostly apparitions remained unmoved.

Random tried to get a better view of them. They looked like completely different species. One was impossibly tall and gangly, with a sapphire blue complexion to its skin tone, the other much smaller and obviously feminine with a crimson red pigmentation.

'I know you've always been with me. I know what you want me to do. But I can't. Not yet. I'm not ready yet.'

Their silence was deafening.

'For zarks sake! Why would you haunt my every waking moment and not speak a word now! What are you trying to prove? Come on! Speak!'

Random attempted to run towards the phantoms but he wasn't able to gain any ground on them. They remained far away in the depths of his mind. Giving up, he stood in the void, feeling overwhelmed with confliction.

Up ahead were two figures that he could barely make out, and if he attempted to move closer towards them, they didn't get any sharper in focus or any nearer in proximity.

'Why? Why are you haunting me?'

The two ghostly figures were unmoved and remained silent.

'Is it something you put in my head when I was created? Are you trying to warn me now? Why won't you answer!?'

Random was becoming more and more frustrated. Anger was bubbling underneath the surface.

'Look, if you've nothing to say then go on, zark off! Leave me alone. I will fight on my own terms, when I am ready, not before. I am not allowing the ghosts of Rodas to bully me into rushing back. I didn't ask to be your saviour. I'm not asking you now and I never will. I'm just asking you, if you are who I think you are, to leave me alone.'

The apparitions stayed totally silent.

'GO!'

With a crushing blow, Random smashed his fists to the ground and awoke from his dream with a startle and in doing so, shocked Anji into a scream.

'Oh my god, don't do that!' she cried out, her heart racing.

Random could feel the sweat pouring down his face.

'Anj! You startled me! Hold on,' he became aware of his surroundings. 'Right, I take it that Lon's got away then judging by our current predicament?'

'Not before he left us here! Still at least we can talk now since we aren't going anywhere. What's the matter, Random, please tell me?'

'Not now, Anj, can't you see we're dangling above a pit?' he said curtly. 'Anyway, I'll be fine, I think it's all sorted now.'

Again, Random was quick to change the subject. 'So, let's look at the facts. We are tied up above what to the naked eye looks like a bottomless pit and we're miles away from safety either side.'

'How did he get us up here?' Anji pondered.

'Never mind that for now, we need to think of a way of getting out.' Random muttered as he fiddled with his bonds.

'Random, listen, it's not just us who are in trouble. Jake phoned me. Auger attacked him in his sleep and left him buried alive!'

Random stopped. 'What!? Where was Skateboard? Were they okay?'

Anji continued. 'He's lost Skateboard, but someone was rescuing him while he was talking to me.'

'Let's hope it isn't Auger then and that
Skateboard is okay.'

'Who do you think it could be? Could it be the
Spectronians?' Anji enquired.

'No, not this far out I wouldn't think. Hold on.'

A look of worry passed over Random's face.

'You said that someone was rescuing him?'

'Yes.'

'Well, if what we've been told is true, then there's
one person we certainly don't want him to be
rescued by!'

*

'Stay away from me!'

Jake pointed accusingly in the direction of his
rescuer. 'I know karate! Ish!'

Strakonis adopted a calming tone. 'You've
obviously been through a lot but I can assure you, I
mean you no harm.'

'Oh yeah, prove it!'

Strakonis held his palms out in front of him. Jake
observed him. He stood tall.

His black leather outfit resembled something
bikers would wear back on Earth. Despite being
apparently well-built, his face and hair were as
white as snow and his hair was thin and long and
moved with every slight movement of breeze in the
air.

'I just rescued you from a shallow grave...'

Jake paused. 'Good point.'

Strakonis pulled the boy up to his feet.

'Now the question is, what were you doing down there?'

Jake hesitated. He didn't want to give away who he was travelling with.

'How can I trust you?'

'Well, I would have thought rescuing you would have been enough to prove it,' he tutted. 'Look if you're going to continue to be evasive then I'll be on my way…'

'That might be for the best…'

Strakonis lurched down and pulled his cloth mask down. Jake shuddered at his terrible facial scars. Dried blood and ligaments were visible in the place where flesh should have been.

Strakonis saw the fear in the young boy's eyes. 'You're afraid of me, aren't you?'

'No,' lied Jake, 'Whatever gave you that impression?'

'Then why hide the truth.'

Because I don't want you to put me back in that hole, screamed Jake's inner voice.

'Look…I've heard of you, and what you do, and I don't want any trouble.'

Strakonis looked confused.

'Tell me…how bad must a man be to dig a live being out from the ground and save their life?'

'I don't know…thank you, by the way,' said Jake sheepishly.

Strakonis was right though. Auger had betrayed him and Skateboard but this man, someone he had been told was evil and perceivably untrustworthy wasn't the one who left him to die a horrible death.

'I just don't know who to trust,' he admitted.

'Come with me. We'll go back to the shack, patch up that jaw of yours and see if there are any clues as to the whereabouts of your friends. I take it from your reluctance to tell me the truth that you were not alone?'

'No, I was with a friend and someone I thought I could trust. Well…ish.'

'Come on,' said Strakonis.

Jake walked with the man he had been led to believe was an evil mastermind like a child following their parent. He was so confused. But Auger seemed okay, he thought, well, until she did what she did to him. So had she and Lon been lying all along?

The burial site was mere metres away from the shack, so Jake and Strakonis were soon entering the tiny building. When Jake saw the familiar outline of Skateboard lying inert in the middle of the dusty floor, he immediately ran to his side.

Strakonis watched on. 'I take it that robot was with you?'

A lump of motionless metal lay before their feet. Jake threw himself towards it.

'Skateboard, buddy it's me,' he said, shaking his lifeless form.

Jake looked all over for life signs, which was a difficult thing to check for a robot. As far as he was aware, Skateboard didn't have a respiratory system.

Normally the little AI would have little lights flashing, or a blue energy flowing through his metal work like blood coursing through veins, but this time, there was nothing. Then as Jake's hand caught the jagged stab wound that gaped open on his back, the full horror of what happened hit him.

'No!' he exclaimed.

Strakonis kneeled down next to the disconsolate boy. 'Let me have a look at that.'

'Get away from him!' railed Jake.

'Look, he's a machine, let me take a look and we might be able to fix him.'

Reluctantly, Jake handed Skateboard, who was surprisingly light, over.

Strakonis inspected the wound and then took a closer look at Skateboard.

'It's pretty bad. His energy pack has been pierced. It will take a lot of work to get him up to speed again.'

'You mean he isn't dead?!' said Jake, allowing a glimmer of hope to enter his world. 'You can fix him!?'

'I don't think I can, but I'm sure the Spectronians can.'

'Well then we've got to get him to them now!'

'No, I'm sorry but I can't go with you.'

Jake frowned. 'What do you mean?'

'There's something very important I have to get back to,' said Strakonis as he pulled his cloth mask back over his mouth.

'More important!' Jake spat. 'My friend is dead!'

'No, he isn't dead. I'm sure there are technicians back at the Spectronian city who can help patch him back up again. But I cannot go with you. I need to make a promise and make my rendezvous. I'm already late as it is.' He made for the shack door.

'But my friends need help too!' pleaded Jake.

Strakonis paused in his tracks. 'More of you?'

'In the mountain, yeah.'

Strakonis shook his head. 'I cannot help, I'm sorry.'

'But you must!'

'Look!' Strakonis snapped. 'It's terrible what's happened to you, I know. And in other circumstances I would not hesitate to lend a hand but there is something in my possession that needs to stay out of people's hands and I can't guarantee that unless I go on now. So I'll help patch you up then be on my way. Now, where's my first aid kit.'

'By "people's hands" do you mean Lon?'

Strakonis turned back and strode up to the scared blonde boy. 'You were with him, weren't you?'

Jake nodded.

'He rescued us when our ship crash landed.'

'A likely story!'

'It's true. And then he invited us to join him. Not the nicest of blokes it has to be said.'

'Was it him who did this to you and your friend?'

Jake shook his head. 'No, that was Auger.'

Strakonis' eyes widened. He spoke in hushed tones.

'So, he's companions are here too, just as I thought…and Lon has endangered your other friends' lives?'

Jake sighed. 'Please.'

'If Lon is not alone then it's imperative that I move as quickly as possible,' he rummaged in his first aid kit and took out a futuristic looking plaster. 'Right, stick this to your wound and allow it to do the rest.'

He got up and delved into his pockets and finally produced a small gadget that Jake presumed was a communicator.

Strakonis held it to his mouth.

'Eago, Eago, this is Strakonis. Found wounded non-native and machine in shack. I am sending you my coordinates now…' he broke off and tapped some buttons on his communicator, allowing his contact to respond. '…Unable to stay…the mission has become a little more uncertain. Lon is in pursuit and it's not known if the traps have worked. Please come quickly, humanoid boy is distressed. Strakonis out.'

'Thank you,' said Jake.

'Sadly it's the least I can do, if I don't get the Flux to our rendezvous point then the fate of the galaxy is in trouble.'

'Lon's pretty determined to get his hands on it.'

'He always is, no matter what we are searching for. Our paths cross more times than I care to remember. Now please, stay here. You'll be safe as soon as Eago gets here.'

Jake gave a weak smile to his rescuer.

'Good luck.'

'Thank you.'

'Oh, one more thing before you go.'

Strakonis stopped in the doorway.

'This Flux thing – do you have it with you?'

'No.'

Jake paused.

'Oh, so I can't see it then?'

'No. Goodbye. I hope you find your friends.'

And with that, Strakonis swooped out of the shack and left Jake to cradle his dead friend, waiting for the promise from a stranger.

*

'Try again!'

With what felt like the umpteenth swing of her legs, Anji tried once again to throw momentum to her right.

She and Random swung like a pendulum, swinging back and forth between the two cliff edges, but always falling several metres short of safety.

'Random I can't keep doing this!' said Anji, afraid to admit that with the height of the drop they were swinging above she was liable to black out as she did climbing the mountain.

'Okay, okay, so we're too far away to jump on the ledge, fine.'

'Can't you just snap the ropes and jump over?' Anji suggested.

'I don't think I am close enough to do that…unless…'

'…Unless?'

'Maybe I can, yes! Anj, if I snap out of these bonds, permission to climb down to your feet?'

'My what?'

'You know them, boney things with toes on the end?'

'Don't be silly, I just don't understand why you'd want to climb down to my toes.'

Random smiled like an excited child. 'Simple. Use your momentum and a longer length span to flip back onto the ledge.'

Anji sighed.

'So it's back to swinging again then?'

'Well it's better than hanging around, come on!'

Random concentrated his efforts in the ropes around his hands.

He began to force them apart, grinding his teeth as the bonds began to strain and pull. Before long, they twanged open. Random beamed as he felt his wrists.

'Got them!'

'Great!'

'Only…'

'Only what?'

'Well, I've just realised. If I snap out of the rope that's tying me to you, you will be free too.'

'What's the problem with that?' asked an incredulous Anji.

'Don't you see? The tension in the rope fits around two bodies, not one. If we do that, you might fall.'

'Oh.' Anji searched inside her head for a solution.

'Okay, I've got it,' she exclaimed. 'Untie my hands if you can. We are both going to have to swing. Do you reckon we will have enough momentum?'

'If we don't, we'll soon know!' Random gulped.

As Random and Anji were tied back-to-back, he found it easy to find his friend's bonds and roughly went about freeing her.

'Ouch!'

'Sorry, tough ropes,' he said.

Before long, her hands were also free.

'Right, hold on to the rope above us and hold on tight!'

Anji did as she was told.

'And brace yourself Anj.'

Anji did the best she could to get a good grip.
'Random, my hands are really sweaty.'

'Then tell them not to be.'

She frowned. 'Not sure how, humans don't work like that.'

'Oh,' Random replied, 'well, just do the best you can. Hopefully this won't take long. Ready?'

'Nope,' she joked.

'Me too,' replied Random. He gave her a nervous smile and went about his work.

He grunted as he tensed his arm muscles. Suddenly the rope burst open and Anji screamed as she felt her weight fall from beneath her and suddenly it pivoted up to her arms. She looked down, panting heavily, as she saw Random had fallen to her ankles.

'Random!'

'Yes, I know sorry I'm a lot heavier than I anticipated. I'll eat salads when we get back.'

'Stop messing around and swing!'

The duo swung from opposite ends, cancelling out their momentum.

'Not that way, the other way! It's making my hands slip!' panicked Anji.

Random shifted his momentum to Anji's movement and before long they were swinging with significant force.

Anji heard a tearing sound underneath her screams. She dared to look above her and noticed that the weight on the rope was causing it to split!

'Random!!'

'Now!'

Instantly, Random hurtled through the air towards the ledge and pulled Anji after him like a kid who was walking upside down holding on tight to a balloon. They flew towards the ledge and with impressive precision; Random threw the lopsided Anji onto the safety of the ledge.

She fell on her front onto the dusty sand, the rainbow flicks of which stuck to her face. Random landed with all the grace of a moose dancing the fandango on ice.

He rolled to the floor, laid on his back and panted hard.

'See, told you it'd work,' he patted Anji on her back.

She rolled onto her back and tried to catch her breath also.

'I'm never doing heights again.'

Random laughed.

Anji allowed herself a chuckle too. Spotting a glimmer of light above them, she pointed skywards.

'Look, there's a hole in the roof of the cave.'

She pointed right above the rope that was descending from a pin point beacon of sunlight.

'That's how Lon must have dropped us down here. We could have climbed up if we'd have seen that.'

'No, thanks, my climbing days are over!' said Anji.

Random smiled.

'That's the trouble with you sometimes Anji, you are always looking down on things. You've got to look up to find a way forward sometimes. '

'Says you!' she scoffed.

Anji sat up and took a look around.

'Er…Random…'

'What?'

'You know those two ledges we saw when we were tied up?'

'Yeah?'

'We're on the one without an opening!'

Random's face fell.

'Oh.'

'Yup!'

'So, we're still stuck, aren't we?'

'Looks like it.'

Random sighed. He was going to have to ask Anji to do it all over again. To soften the blow, he rummaged around in his pocket and produced a bag.

'Mint?'

XVI

'We shouldn't have done that, you know?'

Etherton's conscience was working overtime. Lon's was clearly missing, presumed dead.

'Spare me the guilt trip, will you Etherton?'

The little creature sighed. In all the years he had been with Lon, on and off giving his availability and the mission he was required for, he'd never seen Lon this driven before. Oh sure, he was ruthless, but then it's a big bad universe. But he had never hurt anyone before.

'How far away are we?'

Etherton checked the digital map.

'We're making good time.'

Lon's patience broke. 'That's not what I asked.'

'About two and a half hours away.'

'We can make it in two if we pick up the pace.'

'But…Lon…what will we say when we meet up with Auger?'

'We'll just say that we lost them on the mountainside and couldn't recover their bodies.'

Etherton was unnerved.

'This isn't you, Lon…'

'Isn't it?' he said, turning to meet his aide head on, his face bursting with frustration. 'So what am I then? Go on tell me!'

Etherton cowered. Lon's eyes were burning with madness. 'Well, I don't know, but not this.'

'I've never lost a prize before. Never. Not once in my life. Not at school. Not in life in general. I'm a born winner, Etherton. To lose is not in my nature and I will not lose this one.'

He turned away.

'Not this one.'

'Lon…' said Etherton softly. 'Strakonis isn't as dangerous as you keep making out. He's just a rival.'

'He's more than that to me…and he is to me! Now come on, you're slowing us down.'

'No.'

'What?'

The mole-like Etherton stood his ground. For what to him felt like the first time in his life, he was putting his foot down.

'I will not help you.'

A deep-seated rage began to boil within Lon.

'This is a poorly timed display of defiance, Etherton.'

'I know,' he said, 'but I can't go on with you like this. You're consumed by the Flux.'

'So would you be if you really cared.'

'But that's the trouble, Lon, you care too much! Who cares if Strakonis has it? He won't use it. No one will come to harm.'

'And you think if I had the Flux people would?'

Etherton hesitated.

'You're not yourself, Lon.'

'That's your answer?'

Etherton screwed his fists up by his side. He was shaking, sweating. Trying not to give away just how terrified he was right now.

'When we have worked together before, throughout all these years, we've acted out of personal interest, chased the glory, but this time…people have got hurt. It goes against what I stand for. So yes, in short, that is my answer. You're losing it Lon. You need help.'

Lon had heard enough. He reached for the knife on his belt.

'You're wrong…I don't need help…but you do…'

*

Jake sat patiently in the shack, still clutching the lifeless Skateboard to his chest.

He looked for a clock on the wall and then quickly reminded himself that this wasn't Earth and that he was being silly expecting to see one. Silliness was something he majored in. First class honours in being silly in even the most desperate situations. He checked his phone. It had been half an hour since Strakonis had left and still no word from the Spectronians.

Sat silently in a strange desert, millions of miles from home, is not the best place to be when you've just been buried alive and aligned
yourself with someone who is willing to kill you and your friend to get what they want.

He needed a distraction.

He decided to try Anji again. He'd called a few times and yet no answer. His stomach was knotted with worry, for them and for Skateboard and also for him.

Thankfully this time, she picked up.

'Bit of an awkward time to call, Jake.'

Anj! You're okay then.' he breathed a sigh of relief.

'Well, that depends on what you mean by "okay". We are free, but trapped. So Random's resorting to throwing me to the other side of the cave to escape.

'Hi Jake!' Random chirped.

'Hey mate,' said Jake nervously. 'Is that safe?'

'We'll soon find out.'

'Before you do that, I need to tell you something.' Jake looked down at the stricken Skateboard and sighed heavily. 'Skateboard's dead.'

'What?!' said Random overhearing Jake on the loudspeaker. 'What happened?'

'It was Auger. She did it. She attacked us. Strakonis thinks he can be fixed though, well he seemed optimistic-'

'Wait, hold on, Jake, you've met Strakonis!'

'Yeah! He dug me out of the ground. To tell you the truth, Random, I don't think he is quite the baddie that Lon has been making out.'

Random looked at the rope dangling from the cave roof.

'You think?'

'Well, early indications say we've been hoodwinked!' said Jake.

'Is he still there with you?' asked Random.

'No, he's gone to meet someone. He said he had the Flux with him. But he knows people on this planet and they are coming out to help us…well, if they ever turn up!'

'Random,' said Anji. 'If Strakonis is the good guy then we've been helping out the bad guys!'

'It looks like it, doesn't it?' Random moaned.

'Maybe we shouldn't be as trusting in future.' replied Anji.

'Forget about that now, we've got to stop Lon! Jake, maintain radio…err…frequencies and let us know when you have any updates. Do you think Skateboard can be repaired?'

'He seemed to think so, but the stab wound is pretty bad, even for a robot.'

'Stabbed!' cried Anji. 'When I get my hands on Auger!'

'We'll be cautious,' said Random. 'Okay Jake, keep us in the picture. We'll get out of here and set off in pursuit of Lon. If you can convince Strakonis' allies to help us that'd be great too. We'll still meet in the same place. Just go easy and hopefully we'll be able to revive Skateboard somewhere along the ling, okay?'

'Gotcha…and Random, Anj? It's good to hear your voices again. The last few hours have felt like years!'

'We'll be back together soon Jake, just you wait,' said Random softly. 'Okay, Random out.'

Anji sighed. 'Speak later, Jake, and stay safe!'

'Will do!'

The line went dead.

Jake pocketed his phone again and went back to rocking back and forth, cradling Skateboard, and waiting for his friend's salvation.

Meanwhile, Auger was struggling with her guilt. As she continued her lonesome trek across the desert towards her destination, she continued to grunt through the occasional whimper of emotion.

She had killed them.

Both of them.

The annoying child and his even more annoying robot and for what?

To get her own way?

Hardly an honourable way to dispose of people who were obstacles in the grand plan.

She hated Lon for making her become this; for allowing these strangers to come along with them. They should have said no. Allowed them time to recuperate and then leave. It was a bad idea and now her conscience was stained red. Is this what she was now?

She sniffed and wiped the tears from her cheeks roughly, sand sticking to it like a persistent reminder, if she needed another, of what she had done.

She was also exhausted. That intruding robot had
been right. She had needed the rest. But for her, she
would have to carry this with her.

The pain, the guilt.

Suddenly, her thoughts turned to Random and
the girl. How would she break the news to them?

What would she say?

Lon wouldn't care. She knew that for a fact. Lon
cared for nothing and no-one. Well, except the
Flux.

It had changed him.

Consumed his mind, poisoned every aspect of his
character. Auger knew he had the capacity to be
ruthless. She had seen it. But when it came to
putting people other than himself in danger? This
was a new level and with it, he had dragged her
down too.

Was the Flux really worth all of this?
Immeasurably power, wealth and fame beyond the
galaxy? Notoriety? They would go down in history
for discovering it.

Auger took a deep breath.

It would be worth it.

She would make it worth it.

XVII

A distant sound of galloping broke Jake from his malaise. He gently put Skateboard down on the floor and made his way over to the door of the shack. Peering out into the brilliant sunshine, he could just make out a clan of Spectronians galloping over the horizon.

'Here they come, Skateboard!' he cried jovially. Even if his robotic friend was incapacitated and thus unable to respond, he felt further reassured that their luck was about to change.

As he watched, a group of four Spectronians pulled up outside the shack, dismounted and moored their tamed beats to a post.

The leader of the gang strode purposefully into the shack, straight past Jake and to the stricken Skateboard.

'Uh, hey!' said Jake, a little indignant that the cloaked man hadn't stopped to see how he was.

'Hello!' said a new voice.

Jake allowed the second helper inside. She pulled her face mask down, allowing Jake to see her beautiful features and making the teenager go a little weak at the knees.

'Uh…hi,' he voice cracked a little.

The girl was roughly his height, shoulder length multi-coloured hair that matched her gorgeous complexion and lovely big eyes that he could have swum in for a week.

'And you are?'

'I'm Jake…'

The girl hummed. 'Jake…I've never heard of that race. Do you have a name, Jake?'

Jake chuckled.

'No, that is my name.'

'It's a pleasure to meet you, No.'

Jake's smile evaporated.

The girl held her thumb and finger out like she was encouraging Jake to give her a call.

'But we've just met.'

'Precisely, this is how we greet strangers on Spectronia, No.'

Jake rolled his eyes.

'No, No, Jake is my name, not No!'

'Alright then, No, No, Jake, let's take a look at you, shall we?'

As two more helpers came into the shack and made it over to Skateboard to assist the head of the group, Jake was encouraged to sit on a nearby stool by his new, weird friend.

She knelt in front of him and sat her bag down next to her. She felt for something inside it and produced a small device and proceeded to buzz it around his head.

'So tell me, No, No Jake, what are you doing out here?'

'Is it possible to just call me Jake?'

'I'm sure it is,' she smiled at him, making Jake involuntarily smile back. He winced and held his jaw.

'Looks like you took a nasty blow there.'

The girl delved back into her bag and found a box of what looked like tablets.

'This'll heal the wound. Before I give these to you you're not allergic to asmosaline, are you?'

'What's that when it's at home?'

'That sounds like a no.'

She handed two tiny tablets, round in shape and white in colour to Jake who put them in his mouth and swallowed them immediately.

'What are you doing?'

Gulping, Jake's eyes widened with alarm.

'You're not supposed to swallow them!'

'Then where do I put them?'

The girl gestured to his posterior. Jake nearly choked.

The girl broke out into a wicked laugh.

'It's okay I'm just joking with you. You'll be fine in a few minutes.'

The boy sighed and laughed simultaneously. What a cruel joke to play on a frightened vulnerable individual.

But god, he didn't care.

He was so in love with her he'd have spat them out and stuck them up there himself if it meant she'd marry him that afternoon!

'Sit there for a second and let them do the trick and relax.'

She flashed him another gorgeous smile and got up to go and talk to the group leader, who had appeared to open Skateboard's damaged battery system and was delving into his metallic circuitry like he was playing Operation.

'I didn't get your name?' said Jake.

'That's because I haven't told you yet,' she said. 'It's Row.'

'Row,' Jake swooned to himself. He was going to get the name tattooed in as many places as possible on his person when he got home, if he ever got home.

He wanted to ask what the others were doing to his friend but then thought better of it. He didn't want to be the reason why an operation to revive Skateboard didn't work. What if they slipped and severed a vocal cord? Would Skateboard ever forgive him if he woke up with a lisp!

After several minutes, in which Jake's jaw was completely set and healed, he could bear the suspense no longer.

'Is he going to be okay?' he called over.

'The main operator jumped.

'Careful!' he exclaimed. 'I nearly severed a vocal cord there!'

Row walked back over to Jake.

'It's going to take a little longer than we expected.
Why don't I take you back to base? We can wait for
your friend there?'

'No, I want to stay with him.'

Row placed her hand on Jake's shoulder.

'He is safe now, don't worry, he is in good hands.
Come on, you can ride with me.'

'Okay, actually, I need to see Solenia. Can you
take me to her please? She needs to know what has
happened here,' said Jake hesitantly. As Row led
him out of the shack, he shot a look over to his
broken friend.

'You can get through this, Skateboard. You can do
it mate.'

As he left the shack, Row had already mounted
her stallion.

'Ever ridden a Doa before?'

'If that's what that thing is then I'm afraid not.'

'Hop on.'

Jake approached the beast gingerly and carefully
put one leg over the other and slid into the saddle
behind Row.

The Doa whinnied a little.

'See, she likes you. Now put your hands around
my middle and hold tight.'

Jake blushed. The last time he put his arm around
a girl's midriff, Anji had slapped him. He'd never
had a girl ask him to hold on to her before. Gently,
he reached around her slender waist and locked his
fingers together.

'Here we go!'

The Doa rose in the air and galloped across the soft sand, bouncing Jake and Row up and down as they tore away at great speed away from the shack that Jake was hoping to never revisit in person or in memory. Instead he gave into the momentum of the Doa and let his head like on Row's back and sighed to himself a little.

So, he thought, *this is what heaven feels like.*

XVIII

Meanwhile, whilst their friend was busy falling in love for the first time that day, Random and Anji had finally escaped the boredom of the pit and managed to stumble upon a passageway. The only trouble for the duo was that it was half blocked by a rock fall, so they had spent the last twenty minutes doing their best to clear as much of the rocks as possible and they were now so close to getting through.

'Phew!' said Anji as she wiped her brow with the back of her sleeve. 'First thing I'm doing when I get back to the Venus II is taking a shower!'

'You may have to join the queue!' said Random, whose face was soaked in sweat.

With a final push, they had made it out the other side.

'Finally!' declared Anji.

When the dust had settled they looked out on a clear and unabated path out of the mountain. A glimmer of light appeared at the end of the tunnel and it flooded Anji's outlook.

'Come on! We've got to stop Lon!' said Random. He tore off ahead of Anji and out of view. A purple blur shot away from her, and then shot back up the path towards her.

Without warning, Random grabbed her by the hand and yanked her along with him.

Solenia sat upon her throne, chewing over what the strange blonde boy in front of her had been saying ever since he had burst into the throne room. He had made quite an entrance and accidentally knocked over a priceless vase that was balanced precariously on a plinth next to the main doors.

In doing so, Solenia felt that she was well within her rights to condemn him to an eternity of embarrassing punishments. As soon as she had deciphered the gibberish he seemed to be spouting about being buried alive, a robot getting stabbed and Auger and Lon being murderers, she knew she had to step in.

'Enough of this, we have not a moment to lose,' she said whilst standing up and making her way down towards the frantic boy.

'You have been through much, I implore you to stay here and rest. We will deal with the rest.'

'Your Majesty, I must come with you. My friends will need me.'

Solenia put her hand on his shoulder, and then wished she hadn't with the clumps of rainbow coloured earth and what must have been sweat dirtied her hands.

'As you wish…but we leave immediately. Guards.'

The two golden robed strongmen standing either side of their Queen stood to attention even stronger than they originally were and waited on Solenia's next order.

'Summon the Valkyries. We have no time to lose!'

*

High above the glorious skies of Spectronia, a fleet of mysterious flying pyramids were sailing ominously towards the illuminating planet. Dozens upon dozens of ships continued on their descent in a formation that rather unimaginatively also resembled somewhat of a pyramid itself.

At the tip, apex as it were, was the command centre, the same edifice that Random had escaped not too long ago after failing to get on the good side of the gods who had sat dormant for so long before he had disturbed their slumber.

Now, they wanted revenge.

How was Random to know that gods were also susceptible to being a little cranky after a long snooze?

'The traitor is moving within range,' said Isis.

'Shall we open the laser cannons?' asked Thoth.

'What would be the point from here,' said Horus. 'The target is too far away. We must move in closer. Crush the planet if we must. The traitor must die.'

'Wait!' Ra arose from his throne, dust falling from his frame as it moved for the first time in eons. 'I sense a great power. An orb with enough energy to power a thousand suns, or burn a thousand skies.'

'Ra speaks the truth,' came another voice.

'Bennut, you sense the same power?' asked Isis.

'I can smell it like the most pungent of herbs, it pumps through my blood like a river of lava.'

Ra smiled sinisterly. 'Doesn't it feel good, Bennut?'

'It does…if we destroy this planet before obtaining this amazing power, we could lose the one chance we have of reobtaining our true place as the rulers of the universe.'

'Come on,' tusked Osiris, 'You expect us to believe that? What of the traitor? And if we do obtain the…orb…as you describe it, what makes you think the Syonians won't try to face us again?'

'We could easily crush the insolence of those righteous fake idols once and for all if we had this power, trust me,' smiled Ra. 'Listen to me, brothers and sisters, my fellow deities, this is the chance to gain life beyond immortality. To have the power to give or take life as and when we see fit, this will be a momentous day for the Osirans. It is the day that we can take control of supremacy in every single corner of the cosmos. Not even the furthest, darkest embers of the universe will hide from our supremacy.'

The assembly murmured in agreement.

Ra continued. 'Galaxies can be bent to our will with a mere thought. We must seize the power…and ascend above glory, past myth…all will know of the Osirans, and they will grovel in the dust at the mere thought of our presence.'

'Not without the consent of Amun-Ra,' barked the Mother Goddess.

'I am Amun-Ra!' barked Ra. He was right. Amun-Ra was an amalgamation of the god of war, the very deity trying to wage galactic war on the rest of the cosmos before his peers, and Amun, an almighty god, who was unwilling to merge with Ra since the Osirans had been paralysed and left abandoned in space.

'Amun, show yourself,' Ra demanded.

There was silence in the vast bowels on the ship.

'I will not consent to this,' came a tired voice.

Ra laughed. 'You dare let the opportunity of supreme power through your fingertips?'

From the shadows, a face, human in design, peered through the darkness towards its impetuous rival.

'The universe reeks of megalomania. In the eons we have both lived and been imprisoned by dormancy, countless others have sought to control all living matter.'

'But Amun, we are hundreds in number!'

'Exactly. The quantity of egos in this room negates democracy. We can never agree on anything. You and I are the same creature and we can never see eye-to-eye.'

'Amun, you forget, you need me to break this feeble spell of soul searching. I can handle the call to power but I am asking you to join me in a call to arms…solidarity can lead to our supremacy. Trust me!'

Amun sighed hard.

'Trust…now why would anyone ever trust a god of war? Destruction, devastation, disease. These are all brought about by Kings such as yourself.'

'Well, you did once,' said Ra. His comment cut through Amun's heart.

'I did, and it was a mistake that we must learn from here. No god should be above their peers.'

'No god,' spat Ra. 'But I!'

'Stop him!' cried Isis, but it was too late. Ra's form began to merge with that of Amun's. A brilliant struggle of wills battled it out in a blaze of white fire that enveloped the pyramid ship. Within seconds, the space that had been occupied by the two gods was unoccupied and a larger, bigger being began to emerge from the brilliant light where Ra had been standing. There was nothing left in the vacant spot that Amun occupied. He had been consumed.

The vast creature descended to the floor, huge in stature and resembling little of Amun and more the face of Ra, it glared down upon all the gods of the Osirans.

'Kneel before us…'it boomed its thunderous order. 'Kneel before me.'

XIX

'Lon!'

Auger had never been so pleased to see someone in her entire life. She had picked out the familiar outline of her colleague and ally across the sands and ran to be with him again. Her chance of redemption had just become very real.

It had seemed like forever ago since she left the boy and his talking board for dead – and forever is a long time for one person to be alone with their conscience.

Lon was silent in response. He proceeded to move towards her but in a manner that was as though Auger wasn't even there.

As they got closer, Auger registered that Etherton wasn't with him. Or Random. Or the girl.

'Where are the others?'

Lon continued on his approach, his face drawn and his eyes black with fatigue.

'You look terrible,' she said.

'Noted,' he brushed off the remark as he powered on past her. She turned on her heels and caught up.

'Woah, woah, slow down a second there, aren't you going to ask me what's been going on.'

'No.'

'Lon.'

'Enough.'

Auger frowned. 'What's happened?'

'Nothing's happened.'
'Don't kid a kidder, Lon.'
Lon stopped.
'Kill a killer? Who said anything about killing?'
'No, you misheard me, look I had to get rid of the other two.'
'Good, that's the first sensible thing you have done since you got here.'
Lon picked up the pace again, leaving Auger slightly aghast.
'Excuse me!?'
'Auger I have neither the time nor the patience to carry on with this conversation. I don't care what has happened to your little friends and I ever will, do you understand?'
'Lon, what's got into you?'
'Again with the questions...'
'Well if you are going to treat me like a child then I demand to know why you've gone rotten all of a sudden?'
'All of a sudden? I've always been rotten, Auger. Right to my very core!' he cried. 'If you don't know that about me by now then I doubt we've ever got to know each other in the first place.'
Auger reeled as it dawned on her why her friend was acting like this. She wanted to act out like he was too. That could only mean one thing.
'You killed them.'
Lon's eyes dimmed. He resisted temptation to dignify Auger's claim with a response.

'Look at what the Flux has done to us!'

'We can think about our actions when it is in our grasp, and we are off this zarking planet!'

'I don't think I can live with the guilt...'

'Then after you've helped me retain it, don't.'

Auger was appalled.

'How dare you!' Is that what you really think?'

'I think of nothing but the Flux. The ultimate prize!' he spat.

'It's consumed you! Changed you! The very thought of it has poisoned your mind.'

'You sound like Etherton,' he sighed. 'Your minds are too narrow for ambition. I'm relieving you of your services right now.'

'Lon, you need help!'

'I need the Flux!'

Auger's eyes met with Lons. She saw the madness that now consumed him, the same madness that was the final image that Etherton had seen.

'Leave me.'

'But Strakonis...'

'...is no match for me. Not this time. Not now I know what I am capable of. Go home, Auger.'

Auger let him continue his journey. She was through with fighting with him.

After all these years, this was it. He was beyond redemption. He had killed Etherton and the two Earth kids. She had killed too, but at least she still had her guilt. Lon was without redemption.

He had to be stopped.

As Lon marched towards the canyon, which was quickly appearing on the horizon, he suddenly felt a hot bolt of agony erupt in his left arm. He cried out in pain and crunched down to his haunches. Inspecting his wound, he noticed what looked like a laser injury.

Through gritted teeth, he reached into his boot with his good hand and spun around sharply. Without remorse, without compassion, he fired several shots of gunfire back at his old friend, crying out with all the rage and fire that burned within him until Auger lay motionless in the dust in the distance.

He pitied her. To him she was so close to the prize, but just as weak and feeble as the others when push came to shove.

Lon glared down at the wound. The heat of the laser shot had cortisoned the hole that now lay searing hot near his upper shoulder, so at least he didn't have to stop to tend to it. The determination that burned in his soul wouldn't allow him to do that anyway. Nothing was going to slow him down now.

Lon flicked a small switch on his gun to recharge it. The finish line was in sight and when he got there, he was ready to end this for good.

No one was going to take the Flux from him.

No one.

The canyon was quiet, still. No living being disturbed the silence that hung in the thick, stuffy air.

As venues for a showdown between two ruthless, ambitious explorers battling for the most powerful element in the known universe went, the canyon looked a far from grand.

Strakonis watched from high above at the very top of the canyon, his trap laid and set to obliterate Lon and his cronies as soon as they set foot in the quagmire.

As he replaced his binoculars and reached for his satchel, produced a flat bread snack and he took a sizable bite, he thought about the boy he had encountered in the shack.

He said that he had other friends who needed his help, but Strakonis wasn't able to come to their aid. He'd wanted to.

Strakonis hated the thought of people getting caught in the crossfire of his long running feud with Lon.

Besides, he had the Flux to protect, to hide and if he hadn't made the canyon in time, it would never make its rendezvous.

Suddenly, his thoughts were disturbed by what appeared to be a flash of purple light far below his vantage point.

He reached for his binoculars and gazed down on what looked like a young boy and girl. They were humanoid in appearance, but it soon became clear to Strakonis that his complexion was what had given off the impressive purple hue. This wasn't part of Lon's team, nor did they look like natives. These were the friends that Jake had been talking about.

And then he realised the danger they had just walked into and ran towards a cave opening nearby...

*

Random stopped immediately after he and Anji had finished sliding down a thousand foot-long rainbow, something they did for no other reason than Random thought it looked like fun and just might get them to the canyon quicker than the conventional pathway.

Silent Path? More like the Party Path!

At least Anji had reasoned with herself that they probably would get to the canyon faster that way but giving her new adversity for heights, she'd actually had quite a lot of fun too. She just hoped that Jake, wherever he was, hadn't seen them, otherwise she just knew he would be jealous. She hopped off the rainbow and surveyed the desolate plain.

'Looks like we beat Lon then.'

'Looks that way?' said Random, gasping for breath. 'Right, let's have a little look around. See if this Strakonis is anywhere to be seen-'

As he placed his foot forward, Anji recoiled in alarm. 'Random watch out!'

A barrage of laser fire exploded from a nearby rock, causing Random to throw himself to the side and with cat-like reflexes pull Anji down with him and before she knew what was going on, she was on the ground with him.

'That was close!' said Random as the barrage subsided. As he got up, a rumbling sound filled the canyon. Anji, who remained face down on the floor swore it was getting louder.

Random looked down at his chest and noticed a hologramatic bullseye imprinted on his t-shirt.

Panicked, he grabbed Anji once again and threw the pair of them against the cliff face just as two huge boulders cascaded over the top of the canyon and smashed in the very space they were standing in, sending debris and dust up in the air like a mushroom cloud.

As the chaos settled, Random and Anji put their hands up in surrender, not daring to move their feet anywhere else but from where they were firmly planted.

'Stop! We come in peace!' shouted Random. He turned to Anji. 'Ugh, don't tell anyone I said that!'

'Forgive me,' said a far-away voice.

'Only if you stop attacking us!' shouted Anji in reply. She looked all around for confirmation of where the voice was coming from.

'The failsafe is in operation now. You are free to move around the canyon...if you confirm to me who you are and what you are doing here?'

Random lowered his hands very slowly.

'I take it we are speaking to Strakonis?'

'You are,' replied the disembodied voice. 'And whom may I say I am talking to?'

'My name is Random and this is Anji. You helped our friends Jake and Skateboard out earlier.

There was a moment of silence.

'Hello.'

All of a sudden Strakonis popped up from behind them, making Random and Anji jump like cartoon characters startled by a mouse in old 1960s cartoons.

'I apologise for the less than hospitable welcome.'

'It's alright, we understand why you've gone to such lengths to keep the Flux safe.'

Strakonis surveyed the two strangers. Anji was startled by his appearance.

'Don't be alarmed,' he reassured her. 'Although my appearance is less than palatable I can assure you my offer of friendship is.'

He held his hand out to shake Random's own, with the Rodasian returning in kind by pinching his thumb and pulling it up and down.

Strakonis laughed. 'Yes, well, we all have our customs. Follow me. There is much that I need to know.'

'He's on his way,' said Random grimly.

'I don't fancy his chances against that lot!' said Anji, looking back at the rubble and smoking holes in the rocks.

'You can never be sure with that man, come let us talk inside.' With that, Strakonis led the pair through a concealed opening in the canyon wall and they passed through what to them looked like solid rock.

'Holograms!' said Random admirably.

'Cloaking devices,' Strakonis corrected him.

'Whatever it is it's impressive!' said Anji.

'In my line of work you need it,' replied Strakonis.

The trio snaked up a metal gantry.

'So, I take it this isn't a feature of the canyon, no?' asked Random.

'Certainly not,' smiled Strakonis. At the top of the gantry he pressed a button on the wall. A door slid open unveiling an impressive control room to an aghast Random and Anji.

'Oh wow!' cried Anji.

The place was the stuff of science fiction dreams. A myriad of switches, flashing lights and what looked like important instruments adorned the walls and a black flat table system that sloped ever so slightly up to the ceiling, which was just as dark as the cabin.

'It looks like a Christmas fair in here,' said Anji.

'I'm going to assume that that's a good thing,' said Strakonis. 'Sorry about the mess, when you are forever travelling you don't really have the time to clean up after yourself. Please.'

A bony hand offered Random and Anji to sit down on a large brown sofa. They accepted in kind but turned down their new acquaintances offer of what looked like a very muddy pot of coffee.

'So then,' said Strakonis as he lowered himself down in a command chair that Anji thought looked like a gaming one she had seen in a shop window one time, 'tell me everything.'

'Wait a minute,' said Random, 'it's all very well you being so nice to us after, you know, trying to blow us up and crush us with your traps, and while we understand why you've had to do that, it would be good to know that we are actually on the right side this time. Who's to say that you are not as mad with power as Lon?'

'Because even though I have the Flux I do not want it...and I am making you a cup of coffee. Evil geniuses are not prone to offer hot refreshments, are they?' said Strakonis.

'You don't want the most powerful element in the universe?' asked Anji.

'No,' Strakonis confirmed.

'Then why are you going to all of this bother?'
said Random.

'It's a fair question so I will give you a fair but
fairly obvious response…because I am hiding it.'

'Why?' asked Anji.

'Because the very thought of obtaining the Flux is
enough to turn any being in the cosmos mad. Take
Lon for example. Sure, we are rivals, We go way
back. We've battled throughout the galaxy for
treasure, but the Flux is the one thing any explorer
desires, but should never have. I don't want to be
in possession of it at all. I'm just a courier.'

'Courier for who? And can they be trusted?'

Random wondered who Strakonis might be
working for.

'I believe so. I know so. The Flux should be
protected from any being who desires it. So to give
it to a person who does not want it, and will pretty
much forget about it in the years to come, is more
than safe.'

'But from what Lon has told us it can do so much
good for the universe,' said Anji. 'Put an end to
famine, energy supplies, that's what he said.'

'It's true…' said Strakonis, '…but what if the
person who uses it for that power becomes
corrupted, started using it to take over worlds,
destroy lives? It's happened before, it can never
happen again.'

Then Random thought, somewhat misguidedly, that this would be the best time to ask the question that was on both he and Anji's minds.

'May we see it?'

Strakonis huffed.

'No.'

'Strakonis, we are willing to accept what you are telling us, but without seeing what you are protecting, it's hard for us to believe it's really worth all of this.'

'That's no justification to show you.'

'I know, but I thought it was worth saying.'

Strakonis exhaled. 'Okay, but I must warn you, it does have an immense power, more than many living beings can comprehend.'

'Alright, we promise we won't touch,' said Anji, smiling.

Strakonis got up and made for the control panel. He flipped a few switches and before long a slow, hydraulic tube descended from the ceiling, slowly filling the room in a heavenly emerald glow.

'Behold,' he said, 'the Zedron Flux.'

Anji had never seen anything as beautiful as the Flux in her entire life – and that included her short lived but intense crush on Dylan Scott in Year 7.

'My god.'

Random was unmoved.

'It sure is...glowy.'

'I am surprised, my friend,' said Strakonis.

'Random, don't you think it's gorgeous?' Anji purred as she watched it swirl almost balletically in its casing.

'It is a sight to behold, but I can see what Strakonis is talking about.'

The explorer searched for the truth in Random's red/blue eyes. 'You're not feeling a lure towards it? No lust for power? No yearning for it to put anything right?'

Random had wondered about it. Ever since Lon had described to them what the Flux was, he had been slightly tempted by its power. With the Flux, he would have the ability to end the war on Rodas once and for all. Obliterate Kalor Maloso, slaughter the Crimson Empire and purge the Sapphire Regime until they were nothing but dust. But he was not a god. There were other ways of making peace without taking any more lives. The Flux was not the answer and it never would be.

'It's just an intergalactic pawn,' said Random, moving away from it. 'A weapon to hold and say, "ner-ner-ner-ner-ner, I have it, can't touch me now". I mean, that's pretty sad really isn't it?'

Strakonis flipped a switch and the Flux began to rise back into his housing and the light began to fade back to normal in the cabin.

'Well, now I know I can trust you,' said Strakonis.

'We can help you get the Flux to where it needs to go,' said Random. 'But I would feel a little easier if I knew who it is going to for safe keeping.'

Strakonis nodded. 'It's Solenia.'

XX

Light.

Then darkness again.

Then another flicker of light.

Followed by another blanket of nothingness.

This sequence of events seemed to come and go for Skateboard but for how long he could not work out. In fact, he couldn't do much. There was nothing for him to compute, he found that he was unable to run a diagnostic, think freely, move or even speak. He couldn't even remember what his name was. No memory of what had happened, who he was.

Tiny hints to these questions kept cropping up every time the light flickered into view, before being cruelly taken away from him again and sending him reeling back into the vast deadness of non-existence.

Every now and then the moments in the light felt longer and he was able to piece together little bits of this information. But it still felt quite vague.

He knew he was on an alien world, far from his own. He knew that he had arrived with others, but their faces were faint.

Something had happened to him, he knew that much. Something awful.

Suddenly, he remembered.

The woman with the knife.

She'd stabbed him.

Worse still.

She had killed him.

Skateboard's hydraulics began to whir inside him at an erratic rate.

He couldn't stop himself.

He was having a panic attack.

'Shhhh,' said a soothing voice. 'Keep calm, you're safe now.'

Skateboard continued to wriggle on the work table.

'Jes, I think he is having a panic attack,' said the nice soft voice.

'A robot? Having a panic attack? Must just be a malfunction Dara.'

'Honestly for an AI expert you really lack compassion. He's had a shock, you know robots can suffer shock, surely?'

'Well, yes of course I do Dara but I haven't switched him back on yet!'

Dara looked down at the panic stricken robot.

'Then his battery pack must have finished repairing.'

Skateboard lay there, wiggling from side to side.

The soothing hushed tones that Dara shushed did little to calm him.

'Please, do stay calm, you're safe now.'

With a croak, like his vocal cords hadn't been used in a long time, Skateboard emitted a dry noise from his speaker grill.

'Try not to talk just yet. You've had a big shock. Just stay there and relax.' Dara stood up and looked at Jes.

'You're fine with us my little friend. Your companion is safe and well.'

Companion? Which one? Had Jake made it out alive?

'J-J'

'Yes, Jake, that's the one. He is absolutely fine.'

Skateboard's motherboard breathed a sigh of relief. He began to settle back down, reassured that these people were not trying to finish off the job that Auger had started.

'You'd better inform this Jake person that the robot is back with us,' said Jes.

'He's gone with her Majesty to the canyon, I'm not sure how we can reach him from there,' replied Dara.

'Contact Medical Officer Row, she'll put him in the picture.'

Dara rolled her eyes. 'Sure, Row gets the good jobs.' Although Row was her superior, Dara had been quite jealous of her of late. In fact, it was Row who had trained with her in the same medical teachings, bio and electrical medical engineering, that Dara had attended but only one of them had obtained promotion and with it, greater freedom to roam the up-above surface of Spectronia.

'Put your jealousy to one side for a moment Dara,' implored Jes. 'You'll see the surface soon, I am sure of it.'

'Yes,' said a third voice. 'You can come with me now and tell him the news yourself if you like?'

Jes and Dara turned back to the work station, where their patient was no longer lying down flat but standing up on his back two wheels.

'What do you think you are doing?!' Jes flapped. 'Stay still, you've had a terrible shock.'

'My dear doctor, I know,' assured Skateboard. 'But I'm not about to let an attempt on my life get in the way of what is threatening those of my friends.'

Dara reached for an electric tranquiliser rod.

'No!' said Jes. 'Put that down.' He yanked the instrument from her grasp. 'You know how these are expensive to run! Now I'm telling you, robot-'

'I would prefer if you would call me by my name; Skateboard.'

'Fine,' said Jes, 'Skateboard. I cannot allow you to leave this facility. Not in your condition.'

'But I have no condition. I have fully recovered thanks to you and your colleagues. I am more than grateful, I can assure you.'

'You can assure me even more by staying still and fully recuperating.'

'Jes,' said Dara holding another, less threatening instrument in her hand, 'he is telling the truth; all systems working perfectly.'

'Then what of the shock he was displaying moments ago?'

'I'm a robot – these things change just like the weather. The shock of waking up from death is fleeting for an AI like me, especially when there are more pressing matters at hand. Now please, let me go. I can take your associate with me to keep an eye on me, just in case I have anymore..."wobbly" moments.'

Jes looked at Dara and could tell that she had nothing but extreme keenness to take the robot up on his offer. 'Fine. I hereby discharge you from this workshop but insist that you stay under direct supervision until my assistant deems it necessary.'

'Thank you,' whirred Skateboard.

'No, thank you!' grinned Dara.

'We haven't a moment to lose,' Skateboard declared as he hopped off the workstation and with a metal clang landed abruptly on the floor. 'Transferring to horizontal mode,' he said as he flopped onto his four wheels. 'Please step on my back, miss.'

'What?'

'It's perfectly safe, I can assure you.'

Hesitantly, Dara picked up her medical bag, packed her scanner inside, zipped up the pocket and stepped onto Skateboard's back. She felt a grip bolt the soles of her shoes to the surface.

'Just tucking you in tight, miss, wouldn't want to lose you on route,' said Skateboard. 'Right, off we go.'

With that, Skateboard tore forward a couple of metres and slapped firmly into the ground.

'Oh,' he cried, in a tone of embarrassment. 'Just one thing before we go...can you attach my front wheels back on please?'

*

Jake had had enough of these alien horses... whatever they were.

He had just got to the age where he was no longer conscious of having a squeaky voice that broke every five seconds or that a pretty girl was around.

Just before he left Earth, he felt like he was finally on par with the other boys around him.

Sure, some of them had developed at a rate that saw them hairier than a gorilla, taller than a giraffe and deeper voiced than...some other zoo animal he couldn't think of right now, but out here in the hitherto undiscovered charters of space, he was unique.

He was the blueprint for humanity that other species could look from and say, "this is what the rest of the human race are like," and then, he wondered if this was actually a good thing or not. He wasn't the neatest, best looking or had the highest levels of personal hygiene that many others possessed back on his home world but hey, who was going to find out any time soon unless they went there?

So that took an awful lot of the pressure off him when it came to the way he thought he was looked upon as a person.

He had grown since he had left the Earth some months earlier. Hell, he'd even got some downy fluff on his chest now! Any time now he thought he would probably have to take up shaving! But after thirty minutes of bouncing up and down on a black alien horse that smelt worse than he did after two hours of football practice, his voice was rapidly regressing to its girly, squeaky version.

What was even more concerning was that and he couldn't feel anything in the trouser department anymore.

'How much further?' he squeaked to Solenia's guard. He was holding on to his tree trunk like waist, although his hands kept slipping a little from the large quantities of sweat he was producing.

Jake had been bitterly disappointed when he was told he couldn't ride with Row, or that he wasn't being given his own Doa. But nothing prepared him for the crushing blow that was having to cling to a half-naked man for the journey.

Solenia had only his safety at hand, and he had insisted upon going with them, if for nothing else, so he didn't miss a slice of the action.

Last time out he had felt a little ignored when Random and Anji had faced the Yarvesh back on Genocia.

Sure he was the one who had freed the slaves and got them out of danger, with a little help from others of course, but it hurt a little that they hadn't been around to see him being heroic. Now here he was again, alone without his friends. Well this time he wanted a slice of the pie. This time he wanted to show them he could be just as heroic as they were.

If for nothing else, just to show off.

And if it took a humiliating and less than cool journey that resulted in his spuds getting crushed by the beast he was riding, then he just wouldn't tell them that bit.

'We are not far away now,' cried the Guard.

'Good!'

'Just do me a favour will you, little girl.'

Jake tried to remember that this was an alien he was accompanying, one who could crush him with one swat of his giant, rainbow coloured hand, so let the mix up of gender slide.

'Sure...'

'Please stop digging your nails into my waist, it really hurts.'

Jake embarrassingly recoiled his fingertips from the Guard's flesh.

'That's better.'

Blushing, Jake fell silent and decided not to speak again until they got there...

In the not-so-far-distance, he could have sworn he saw two familiar looking people sliding down a long and fun-looking rainbow into the cavern.

Jake sighed to himself. Of course Random and Anji would choose the cool route in and he was lumbered with He-Man and his stupid alien horses! Then he thought to himself how cool that sentence sounded in his head and left it at that.

XXI

Auger lay still where she had fallen.

Unmoving, quiet. All for the heavy cries of pain and sobbing.

There was no one around to help her, no one to hear her.

She was well and truly alone.

She tried to move her leg again. Apart from a sensation of searing agony, she felt nothing.

This was how it was going to end for her.

She would bleed out, alone on the most beautiful planet she had ever seen.

And how had she treated her time on this blessed world? Instead of finding the wonder of it all, she had been consumed with nothing else but the drive to reclaim the Flux. Not that they had ever had it. And it had led her to kill, something she had never thought she would ever do, no matter how desperate the situation.

She loathed herself.

This was the end that was right for the person she was now.

To die alone, without comfort or companionship was her punishment...and she deserved every last second of it.

She peered up for a moment, trying to make out Lon in the far distance. He was now but a dark spec on the horizon, no bigger than her thumb.

Someone had to stop him.

But what if there wasn't anyone? What if Lon would end up taking the Flux and becoming ruler of the universe?

She couldn't let that happen.

No.

She wouldn't let that happen.

With great effort, Auger rolled herself on to her side. With a cry of agony, she hauled herself upright. She heaved when she looked down on what was left of her leg. Calming herself, she ignored her wounds, the pain, the blood and with a yell got up onto her feet...well, the working one.

Grunting heavily, she dragged her broken body towards Lon's outline. The sweat cascaded down her face but she ignored it, focusing more on the pain and letting that drive her forward.

She would die today...but not before she had saved everyone else.

*

'So Solenia is on her way?'

Anji studied the orange illuminating map that adorned one of the walls in Strakonis' ship.

'If we are lucky, she will be here in a matter of minutes.' he replied, putting his guests empty coffee cups in a nearby sink.

'Good, let's hope Jake and Skateboard are with her,' said Random.

'But Solenia told us she knew nothing of the Flux,'
Anji pointed out.

'That's because Lon was with you. I had pre-
warned her of his intentions.'

'Then if that's the case, why let us all go in the
first place?'

'Good question Anji,' said Random.

'Believe you me, I wish she hadn't, but my best
guess is that because she was unaware of what his
intentions would be...and technically, his team and
you lot, were not deemed dangerous, she must
have thought she'd chance it by letting you all go
and beating Lon to the prize, as it were.'

'And seeing you safely off this planet?' asked
Random.

'No, the Flux was to remain here, hidden from the
universe. Spectronia is a jewel in the stars of this
galaxy but it is seldom visited or found. My plan
was to leave the Flux with the Spectronians and to
get away before Lon could find me. Sadly, my ship
crash landed. I am stranded here, for the time being
at least. There was no guarantee that my ship
would be ready in time before Lon got here. Plus I
can't keep running from him forever.'

'Is there a way that we can destroy the Flux?' said
Random.

'I have pondered that every day since I
discovered it...well...saved it from Lon's
possession. Unfortunately no. I wish there was a
way but there isn't. Even if you were to throw it

into a singularity, the Flux would only make the
 black hole stronger and consume all of the life in
its wake.'

'Oh great, so it's indestructible then!' Anji threw
her arms up in the air.

'You could say that.'

'So what makes you think Solenia won't be
consumed by it?' said Random.

'She is not concerned for its power. The
Spectronians are a peaceful race. This planet is left
alone by the cosmos. It's remote, hard to find and
so will the Flux if it stays here.'

'Well, we all found it,' said Anji, unconvinced that
the Flux could be hidden successfully. Suddenly, a
blip on the map distracted her attention. 'Hey guys,
there's another blip.'

Strakonis and Random went over to join her.

'Lon,' said Strakonis, who without hesitation
made for his gun.

'And another, fainter one behind him. Who could
that be?' asked Anji.

Random frowned. 'Could be Etherton...or Auger,
come on Anji, we've got work to do.'

'Like what?'

'We've got to buy Strakonis time, stop Lon from
entering the canyon.'

'How?'

'Any means necessary,' said Strakonis.

Random saw the panic in Anji's eyes. 'We are not
killing him!?'

'No, we are not,' reassured Random.

'I would not ask you to do that, that is not a cross for either of you to bear,' said Strakonis. 'But you must do what you can to stop him from getting in here. Let the traps do their job and if they fail, or he finds a way past them, that's when we need to strike, I'll inform Solenia through our communication channel.'

Anji pointed at the scanner. 'Look, Random, there's another blob on the scanner...it's really fast!'

Random grinned. 'That's Skateboard.'

'How do you know?'

'Oh, I know alright! Strakonis, the Spectronians are still further away than Lon, can you tell them to speed up a bit?'

Strakonis threw his microphone down in frustration.

'There's too much interference, I'll have to drop the cloaking device to get through to them.'

'Right, you do that, Anj, let's go.'

All three of them went about their work. As Strakonis dropped the cloaking controls and followed Random and Anji out of the room, a large cluster of blobs began to descend on the scanner. More and more appeared, completely unnoticed.

Before long, it was going to be hard to ignore that they were there. Especially with what the unnoticed intruders had for the people below.

*

Lon had found a way inside the canyon. Squeezing between what should have been a blocked off area, he had instantly found a chink in Strakonis' armour. It looked as though something – or someone – had blasted between the rock face. Fragments of jagged debris lay strewn all about his feet. As he placed his hands on the sharp boulder, he failed to notice that the razor sharpness had made two lacerations in the palm of his hands, like paper cuts right across the flesh. But such was his want, his drive, his mind had told him to ignore it.

*

High above, Random, Anji and Strakonis took up their places and watched like spectators in a stadium as Lon entered the playing field.

'What do we do, drop rocks on his head?' asked Anji.

'Good idea!' chirped Random.

Strakonis readied his gun. 'I can end this here and now with one squeeze of the trigger.'

'No you can't. I haven't known you long Strakonis but I can already tell that you are not a killer.'

Random was right. Strakonis hated him for it but also secretly thanked him for his perspective. He couldn't stoop to Lon's level – he'd never do that. No, he had to stop him by other means.

'Okay, you win, Random. I'll go back to the ship and set up guard there.'

'Are your traps reset?' asked Anji.

Strakonis said nothing.

'Well?'

Without a word, Strakonis legged it back to his ship. The cloaking device mechanism had turned off the defenses also!

'Anj, try and slow him down,' said Random as he pegged it after the explorer.

Anji turned away and looked back over into the canyon. Lon was coming up to the very spot where she and Random were nearly fried by the concealed laser gun.

Nothing happened.

She turned away, desperately searching for something to throw. Quickly, she ran her hand along the ground, picking up chunky nuggets of gravel and started to rain them down upon Lon. But even as the timid rock fall cascaded at him from the sky, Lon did not look up. In fact, Anji didn't even think that he had blinked.

She looked around for more rocks and decided it might be a good idea to move onto slightly bigger missiles. She began to throw fist sized rocks, but her aim was less impressive than the cluster she had chucked over the edge before and they all missed Lon.

The power-crazed explorer had spotted Strakonis'
ship. He started to run towards it, his legs carrying
him ever closer towards the vessel that might, no,
MUST contain the Flux.

'Random!' shouted Anji. 'Plan A didn't work.
Move to Plan B!'

Random could hear the cries of his friend but he
was too engaged in making it back to the ship
before Lon. But Lon had an almighty advantage as
the entrance he had found to the cave was much
closer to the ship than either he or Strakonis were.
Even with his super speed, they still didn't stand a
chance in getting there first.

Strakonis lagged behind, fiddling with his
weapon as Random tore on ahead. He had to get
there first, he just had to.

Throwing himself down the gravel path, he
tumbled as he reached the higher point of the nose
cone of the spaceship. And as he slipped close to
the rocket section a bolt of laser fire embedded
itself into his stomach, sending the Rodasian falling
well over the cliff edge and plummeting towards
the ground.

Anji screamed in terror as she witnessed
Random's lifeless form fall to the ground and with
a sickening thud, he fell at the feet of a grinning
Lon.

'No!' she hollered. 'You murderer!'

Lon looked up and fired his gun in her general
direction.

Anji ducked behind a boulder and felt the heat of the fire shoot past her head and blow a hole in the rock face behind her.

As Lon made for the gantry up to the control room, Strakonis threw himself at his rival and the pair grappled for supremacy. Lon's eyes were as black as his soul as he landed several blows upon Strakonis' person, the protector of the Flux being far from a physical match for his enemy.

Lon punched him again, splitting what was left of his scarred lip. Gripping him tightly by his collar, Lon pulled Strakonis close.

'You thought you could stop me? ME! I was always going to defeat you, Strakonis. You couldn't run from me forever.'

Strakonis spat. 'You haven't won yet...I don't see the Flux anywhere.'

'You're going to tell me where it is and you will do it now.'

Strakonis stared defiantly.

'No.'

Lon landed another devastating blow to Strakonis' badly scarred cheek, sending the beaten man hurtling to the floor. Lon instantly picked him up again but his collar, half choking him.

'You will show me where it is!'

Strakonis began to black out. Only the pain of Lon digging his fingers into the scar tissue on his face kept him awake.

'Or I will finish the job I started a long time ago...'

Strakonis' breath became heavy with anger. So Lon was responsible for the acid attack that mad mutilated him on Ulsamaynor.

'You...'

'Come on, in we go,' Lon dragged the injured Strakonis inside the spaceship, leaving Random lying injured, a trickle of purple blood flowing from the back of his skull.

As Anji raced to his side, she could hear the approaching sound of hooves. She tried not to pay attention to them as she made for the lifeless body of her friend.

XXII

Jake was one of the first to see his friend lying in the dirt. Without hesitation, he dismounted his steed and fell in a crumpled heap on the floor before running to be by Random's side.

'Anj!' he cried.

'Jake! He's fallen, Lon's inside with Strakonis!'

'We'll see to him,' said Solenia. 'Legion!'

A dozen or so guards readied their spears, which all spouted a blue energy ribbon around the spikes in unison, dismounted their Doas and ran towards the ship. At exactly the same time, on Solenia's mark, all of them were thrown with great force away from the ship and landed in an undignified heap.

'Lon must have activated a force field,' said Jake.

'Never mind about that Jake, help him!' cried Anji. She cradled her friend's head and noticed the blood on her hand.

'Oh my god.'

'Stand back,' said Solenia.

'No!' screamed Anji.

'Don't defy me, little girl.'

'You're not my Queen and you won't tell me what to do!'

'Guys, please, don't shout I've got a terrible headache,' murmured Random.

Anji breathed a sigh of relief and held her friend tightly to her in an embrace.

'Ouch, not so hard, Anj, I've got a tummy ache now too. Falling from that height will give you more than butterflies, I'm telling you now.'

Random pushed her away and inspected the wound to his stomach. 'Ah, that explains it.'

'What happened?' asked Jake.

Random, still dazed by his great fall, felt it was better if he mimed a complete guide to his fall, complete with sound effects and hand signals. If for nothing else, it would help him discover the words in his vocabulary that he had momentarily lost after hitting his head.

'…and now here I am but let's not concentrate on that. Where is Lon?'

'Inside. He's got Strakonis,' said Anji.

'Ah. That's not good.'

The hubbub surrounding Random's improbable survival was shattered by a large, pointed shadow enveloping the canyon and a deep humming noise echoing all around. Suddenly, another shadow descended and then another and another. Within moments there were many flying pyramids hanging in the air. If it had not spelt as much danger as it did, Random and his friends would have been impressed.

Anji, Jake, Solenia and the Spectronians were aghast, unable to utter a sound.

'Ah,' Random finally said. 'Neither's that!'

The pyramids swirled in the sky, high above them.

'Who are they?'

'Osirans,' said Random.

Solenia recoiled.

'I thought that they were just legend.'

'Evidently not,' said Random.

'What are they doing here?'

Anji and Jake gave each other a knowing look.

Random knew what he must do. He had to tell the truth – no matter the consequences.

'Your Majesty, I don't think I have the heart to tell you, but they were chasing us across space.'

'So you lied…' Solenia gritted her teeth, a quiet rage slowly building within her.

'Please, we can deal with this some other time, but first we need to rescue Strakonis and deal with the Osirans.'

He was right. Random had also been proved as a liar. But Solenia knew they had to attack two problems now…and the fate of her people, her very planet, hung in a balance.

She had heard of the myths surrounding the Osirans as a child, back in the old times of the Spectronian people, when her Mother read her the stories at bedtime.

She remembered how terrified they made her, sometimes to the point that she'd ask her to stop and read something with a nicer ending.

She had comforted herself at that young age that
these were just stories, and the baddies in those
particular books did not exist.

Now here they were, very much a reality.

'This is your Emperor speaking.'

A deep voice emitted like a sonic boom from the
lead pyramid.

'There is only one ruler of Spectronia,' Solenia
screamed back.

'Solenia,' whispered Random. 'Keep them talking,
stall them.'

'What are you going to do?' asked Anji.

'We are going to break into Strakonis' ship.'
Random got himself up to his feet, with a little help
from his friends who steadied him.

'Good luck...' he nodded at Solenia.

Solenia's warriors grew closer towards their
Queen. 'Who am I addressing?'

'You have the privilege of speaking to Amun-Ra,
Emperor of the Osirans. I care not for who you are.'

Solenia sighed indignantly. 'Well you should. You
are trespassing my world.'

'We are gods. We can go anywhere we like
without prosecution.'

'This is a peaceful planet, we have nothing to give
you, so if you could just be on your way-'

'Oh, but there is something in your possession
that we must have. Our scans detected it, far away
from your world and we will not leave your world
until we have it.'

Solenia looked nervously over to the trio of aliens who had brought this threat to her planet. The purple one was walking around the landing haunches of the ship with a large stick. How she wanted to wrench it from his hands and beat him with it.

'What if we refuse?'

There was a pregnant pause from the pyramid.

'You can protest, you can fight us, you can appeal to our better side but you will do nothing but prolong your agony and suffering…I will not give you further time and this will be the last time we ask you. We must have the element…and we will take the element. It is your choice whether you live to serve us…or die for having the sheer audacity for standing in our way.'

Solenia's guards shivered. The air turned cold. There was nothing they could do but fight. Somehow. Buy the liar's time.

Solenia looked over towards Random once again and glared. He had brought death to Spectronia.

XXIII

With another vile blow Strakonis flew across the
control room and slammed painfully into the
scanner wall, puncturing a hole in the glass and
splintering it to pieces. He fell down.

'Where is it?' I will turn this place to pieces if you
do not tell me!' Lon landed another savage blow on
Strakonis' body, this time cracking a couple of ribs
with his steel capped boot. He began to cough
violently, a coppery taste developing in his throat.

'Have it your way!' Lon left him reeling on the
floor and began to trash the place, pulling tables
and chairs about, tearing things off the wall. The
resistance the stricken man had offered was pitiful
and Lon's attention turned back to his prize.

'Lon, Lon please, for zarks sake open up.'

A voice from outside came over the comms
system.

'You don't fool me, Random,' spat Lon as
Strakonis lay panting on the floor.

He screamed as yet another potential hiding place
again threw up nothing. Desperately, he picked up
a large shard of glass that lay on the floor next to
the crumpled Strakonis. Towering over him, he
pressed the sharp fragment against his jugular.

'This is your last chance…where…is…it!?'

'Lon…you can break every bone in my body, kill me in the worst way imaginable. For the peoples of the universe, to save trillions of lives, I will never…ever…tell you.'

With a fell swoop, Strakonis slashed a similar piece of glass at Lon's stomach, making the crazed explorer recoil in agony. As quickly as possible, Strakonis crawled to the button that turned the force field on and off.

'Random…quick!' he cried before losing consciousness and falling to the floor. But in doing so, the injured archaeologist had brushed his arm against the lever that hid the Flux. Lon was breathing heavily in pain but had noticed that the control room was slowly flooding with a similar green hue that he had seen on the planet Druis.

Finally, Random, Anji and Jake were aboard the ship.

'Quickly!' said Random as they began to tear up the gantry to the control room. But before they had a chance to make it halfway up, the ship began to move.

'We're taking off!' cried Anji.

'We must stop him…the ship might not be ready to take off yet! It could disintegrate if its systems aren't fully regenerated,' said Random, steadying himself and continuing the climb.

'Meaning?' asked Jake.

'Boom!' cried Random.

The roar of the engines sounded very wrong indeed. 'See what I mean?' said Random. Eventually they made it to the top and tore into the control room but the green light was now flooding the ship.

They had failed.

There, standing victoriously, was Lon, with the Zedron Flux in his hands.

*

Amun-Ra had had enough of Solenia's silence. To kill after so long was a lust too strong to resist.

'As you wish,' he said, the words dripping with malice.

'Get down!' cried Solenia.

Suddenly, bolts of green energy fizzed towards the Spectronians, but they all did well to avoid the initial volley of fire, despite a handful of Valkyries being thrown from their horses.

'Take cover!' screamed the Queen as the shots continued to relentlessly pound towards them, thumping into the ground and sending Spectronians and Doas sprawling.

*

Not far away, the chaos had stopped Skateboard in his tracks. Dara stared in horror as the pyramids hung in the sky, raining down death from above.

'The Osirans,' said Skateboard.

'Who?' asked Dara.

'The gods in the pyramids...they found us.'

Dara looked on, tears forming in her eyes as she heard the cries of her people. 'They are killing them...what are we going to do?'

Skateboard scanned for lifelines. He couldn't find his friends, but the people of Spectronia were in clear danger.

'We must act quickly. Get ready to hop off when I give you the word. We must save them.'

Skateboard's wheels span as he propelled himself towards the death zone.

*

Lon starred in total fascination as the Flux twinkled majestically in its holding cell. He started to chuckle, softly at first before descending into a laugh that chilled Anji and Jake's bones.

'Lon,' said Random, who tried to edge towards him, 'Okay, you win. You have the Flux. It's yours. So let's call this whole thing quits, yes? We don't want to take the Flux from you now. But I urge you, you have to use it well and do you know where you should start?

Do you know the first thing that you should do as the supreme ruler of everything? Listen to me. Those people out there need your help. They are being murdered by gods who dare challenge your claim to that thing. Will you allow that?'

Lon said nothing, totally hypnotised by the power he held in his hands.

'Will you?' Random asked again.

'No.'

Random smiled. 'Good.'

'No, I will not help them.'

Random's smile fell.

Strakonis continued to move closer to Lon, out of sight to his bitter rival, but his activity had been spotted by Random. If he could keep him talking...

'Why not?' he asked.

'What's the first thing a man should do when no one around helps him in the first place? He should help himself!' Lon's eyes were manic, possessed.

'Lon, you can't escape. The ship is falling apart. Its engines aren't ready yet. There is no escape.'

'But there is!' he spat. 'As long as I have this! No one can tell me what to do. No one. These gods you speak of...they are not gods...I will make them bow before me.'

With a swift swipe of his shard of glass, Strakonis split the skin across Lon's shins. He screamed in agony and dropped the Flux towards the floor.

In the blink of an eye, before Anji or Jake could act, Random had swooped downward and collected the Flux's cell before it shattered on the cold metal floor.

Suddenly a laser shot burst from the open gantry door, sending Lon sprawling against the wall.

Anji and Jake screamed ducking for cover and looked towards the door.

There, propped up against the frame, her pistol shaking in her hand, was Auger. Her face was broken with emotion as she fired the gun again, burrowing another hole into Lon's chest. A small flame lit his clothes on the outside of the impact and the fallen explorer began to slide down to the floor.

Lon knew he was finished. He had been betrayed at the last by his oldest friend. He had found Auger on her home world and asked her to accompany him on his explorations throughout the cosmos. They had a history that stretched back throughout the decades.

The things that they had seen, the things that they had done.

It all ended like this.

With his dying gaze, Lon looked towards the harsh glow of the Flux.

He ignored all else inside the room.

His rival.

His executioner.

The three strangers he had taken with him and had ultimately played their part in his end.

All faded to black except that luscious, glorious emerald glow.

It was the last thing he saw, the only thing that accompanied him to his end and it was his. It would always be his.

With one final effort, Lon smiled. And then he was gone.

Auger, whose tears were already streaming down her face, sobbed ever more aggressively as she too sunk to the floor. Jake kept his distance from her but Anji kicked the gun from her hand across the floor.

'I had to do it...I had to,' she wailed.

'It's done now,' said Anji.

Random placed the Flux under his arm and turned the ship's engines off before going over to Lon's lifeless body. He placed his fingers on his wrist. There was no pulse. Slowly, he closed the explorer's eyes and then went over to Strakonis.

'Jake, give me a hand.' The teenager went to the aid of the stricken archeologist and placed him gently on a chair.

'I had to do it,' Auger repeated again.

'To make up for what you did to me?' said Jake coldly.

Auger nodded. 'To redeem myself...to save you all.'

'Well I'm sorry but I am not in a forgiving mood,' he replied. Jake replied defiantly.

'I thought I was doing the right thing.'

'How sick must you be to think burying someone alive is right!?' screamed Jake, tears forming in the corners of his eyes.

'Jake!' Random pulled him back with his free hand. He looked his young friend in the eyes. Jake seemed to know what he was thinking. He had been treated horribly, left for dead, but they could deal with that later.

'I know what she did to you was bad but there are people out there who need our help, can you keep it together for just a little longer?' asked Random.

Jake sniffed and nodded his head.

'Good man,' said Random patting him on the back. The Rodasian made for the woman lying wounded on the floor.

'You will have to pay for what you have done.'

'It's too late to kill me...I'm already dead.'

'I'm not a killer. Unlike you. Nor will I thank you for saving us just then. You will not find redemption at our door. When this is over we will hand you over to the nearest penal colony and see to it that you never find freedom again.' he continued.

'I don't think you heard me,' she smiled.

Anji noticed that she had been clutching a deep laser wound in her stomach.

'I have made my amends...' she said, her voice getting weaker.

She looked at Jake, relieved that she had not taken his life and smiled; a gesture that chilled Jake to the bone.

Despite the deplorable things she had done, Anji was finding it hard to hold back the tears. As was Jake, much to his surprise. Random watched as life ebbed away from Auger's features and she too was gone.

Putting the Flux down, Random scooped up his two friends and held them tight to him. He let them cry on his shoulder, he could feel their tears through his t-shirt and he didn't want to let them go.

'I am so sorry you both had to see that,' he whispered.

Anji and Jake hugged him harder.

'I'm never putting you two through this again. Ever.'

Strakonis sighed hard to himself. Despite his injuries, he knew he would be okay in time. But he worried for the three youngsters in front of him. To see such atrocity at such a young age, what would that do to them now? He then looked over at his fallen enemy. Lon was dead. The Flux was safe, until he remembered it wasn't.

'I'm so sorry all of you but the pyramids...the Spectronians!'

Random broke away. 'You three stay here.'

Anji wiped her eyes with her sleeve. 'Where are you going?'

'I'm going to use the Flux against the Osirans.'

'You can't, you don't know what it will do!' said Jake.

'I'm not going to use it really, just as a bluff, I swear.'

'We can't stay here. Not with these two,' said Anji pointing to the corpses. 'I'm going out there to help the Spectronians.'

'It's safer in here!' cried Random.

'It's what we do, isn't it? We help where we can.' said Jake.

Random sighed. 'Okay, but stay as close to the rock edge as you can! Whatever happens, don't wait for me. Find Skateboard and go back to the Venus II, you got that?'

They both nodded. 'Be careful,' said Anji.

'Not as careful as you two,' he shot them a reassuring grin as they both tore down the gantry out towards the chaos outside.

Random could hear the laser fire outside and could not believe he had led his friends to danger again. All for what?

To satisfy his needs?

To distract him from the voices of those two...strangers in his head?

Next time, he'd let them stay on a holiday planet for as long as they wanted.

No.

Next time, he'd take them straight home.

This wasn't a life for them. How selfish of him it was to think he could keep them with him.

'Random,' said Strakonis, struggling to his feet.

'Easy Strakonis.'

'No, I'm fine, I'll mend, Listen, I can use the ship's laser cannons to fight off the pyramids. The nose section of this craft envelops onto the canyon edge. Go up there, it'll keep you out of the fire.'

'Okay, thanks.'

Random made for the door.

'And Random?'

The Rodasian turned back.

'Yes?'

'Whatever you do. Make sure it is a bluff.'

Random nodded.

He would…unless he was left without any other option…

XXIV

Row tried desperately to stop the flow of blood but it was no use. A young Valkyrie was lying on the ground, his eyes vacantly gazing skywards, unmoved. With a grunt of terrible resignation, she threw the stained swabs to the ground and looked around. There were many Spectronians who lay strewn across the canyon like a sea of fallen dominos. She witnessed yet another blown sky high by laser fire.

All this death.

All of this destruction.

She'd seen too much.

'Over here!' came a cry over her shoulder.

Another Valkyrie was being tended to by a comrade, his legs bleeding a sea of rainbow colours.

Row dodged the fire and the shards of rock blowing up all over the place and skidded to the ground to be next to the stricken man.

'I can feel them,' he said reassuringly, 'But, the pain!'

Row turned to his friend. 'Get him behind that rock, now!'

With a struggle, the pair lifted the injured man upright and guided him to a large rock that was roughly ten metres away.

As they got close, they dived for cover again as the shots from the pyramids blew them off their feet.

Row set to work quickly, producing a roll of gauze from her backpack. As she tended to her patient, the other Valkyrie fired back with his electric lance, but the range was just too short.

'They should come out and face us like real warriors,' he muttered.

'They are not warriors; they are gods.'

'Who are you?' asked the Valkyrie to the odd looking robot and his female friend.

Skateboard and Dara had arrived and were ready to do their bit.

'We are friends.' Skateboard reassured.

'For now at least,' Dara said to herself whilst sending a glaring look at Row.

Skateboard noticed the friction and made for a brief introduction. 'Dara, miss, err?'

'Row. I helped you and your friend back in the shack.'

'I'd wish to formally thank you but we simply do not have time. We have to get you all out of the canyon. Dara, show Row the way we got in.'

'Hold on, I'm supposed to stay with you,' Dara reminded him.

There simply isn't time miss, now please. I've got to find my friends and put a stop to this before anyone else gets hurt. Now go. I'll cover you.'

Skateboard produced a little laser gun from his body work.

'Now!' he shouted as he fired off rounds that projected far past the Valkyrie's lance and penetrated one of the pyramid's hull.

'Can we swap?' asked the Valkyrie.

Skateboard didn't have time for banter. 'Go!'

'Right, I'll go pull them out, you girls get moving!' The Valkyrie bravely disappeared back into battle as Dara and Row helped their patient out of the canyon.

'I'm Row by the way,' said Row.

Dara stared indignantly at her. After all these years of being together in the same academic institutions. She had never taken the chance to even acknowledge her existence?

'Unbelievable!' said Dara back.

*

Anji and Jake ran as fast as their legs would carry. They found shelter under a small lip in the cliff face and surveyed the horror around them.

'We've got to get these people out of here,' said Anji.

'How? Where?'

'Anywhere but here Jake!'

Tiny blue shots of light shot skywards towards the pyramids, causing several explosions far away in the underside of the crafts.

'I wonder what caused that?' said Jake.

With precise timing, Skateboard burst into view.

'Yes!' cried Jake. 'Skateboard you legend!'

'Anji, Jake, no time to speak. Where is Random?'

'He's going to bargain with the Osirans,' said Anji.

'Good. Hop on board. We need to collect as many people as possible.'

The two teenagers did exactly as they were told.

'Pick up who you can,' the AI robot implored.

'Not much room, mate,' said Jake.

At which point, a second length of board shot out of Skateboard's back area.

'Don't tell sir that I keep my back up board there,' he said sheepishly.

Anji and Jake didn't have time to make a smart arsed response as they began to hold out their arms and help those stranded in the gun fire onto the board. After two Valkyrie had been collected, Anji notified Skateboard that they had run out of room.

'Blast,' said Skateboard who then headed for the exit, passing Dara and Row in the process. Jake's head swivelled and at the same time a divot on the floor made Skateboard's passengers rock uneasily.

Jake looked down and wondered why he was hurtling through the air whilst everyone else was still on Skateboard's back and getting further away.

Then he remembered how he'd forgotten to tie his laces again.

As he coughed, picking himself up, he looked upwards as a volley of laser fire headed his way.

'You can't kill me!' he cried, 'I haven't got any shoes on!'

A hand shot out and grabbed him by the arm, hauling him out of danger's way.

It was Row.

'H-hi!' he stammered.

'Jake! Where are your shoes?'

'Um...'

'Never mind! Get as many people out of here as you can!' she ordered.

'Yes, that's what I was doing,' he insisted.

'Then keep at it!'

She ran off into the dust again.

Jake looked up and could just make out in the distance the outline of Random, his silhouette bathed in a green light, jumping from the nose cone to the canyon ridge.

'You give them hell, mate,' he said to no-one in particular as he ran back into danger, crying out in discomfort as the broken rock hurt the soles of his feet.

*

'This is sport!'

Amun-Ra gazed out of the ancient viewer and watched with glee as destruction continued to rain down on the Spectronians.

'Change of plan. I am done with the pragmatic approach. Prepare the Armageddon beam!' he roared.

The gods did as they were told. The Armageddon beam was a link between all pyramids that when their energies met, had the ability to split a planet in two with its power.

'We'll fragment this world and obtain the element when we pick it out of that woman's cold dead hands!' he gleed.

'Amun-Ra, look!' came a voice from the dark.

The war god's attention diverted towards the image of a small purple boy carrying what looked like the element they so wanted, standing alone on the cliff top.

'So...another challenger...'

'He has the element, sir!' came the voice again.

'Not for long...cease fire...for now. Create the energy link.'

*

Mercifully, the lasers stopped. Solenia, who was flat on her back, let the dust and the eerie calm wash over her before struggling to her feet. Jake and Row rushed to her side and tried to help her up but she was adamant she could help herself. Apart from a cut on her forehead, she looked fine.

All three of them stood and watched as the pyramids began to hum.

And on the cliff top, all alone, facing them down was one boy.
    Random.

XXV

'Who dare faces us?'

The voice boomed out of the head pyramid.

Random stood defiantly.

'Don't you remember me?'

There was a pause.

'You...'

'Yes, me,' he said lightheartedly. 'I didn't have supposed god down as being short on memory. Short on brains perhaps.'

'You dare mock the Osirans!'

'I do!' he shouted. 'Because you dare to take what isn't yours and destroy a people you know nothing about.'

The canyon fell silent. Anji and Skateboard rushed to be by Jake's side. They were all glued to what was happening high above.

'You have the element.'

'Oh, this?' Random said, swigging the Flux to and fro in his hands. 'This old thing? Well I suppose you could call it an element. If you don't know what it is in the first place.'

'It is the most powerful element in the known universe.'

'It's called the Zedron Flux, look it up in your history books and yes, I suppose it is.

In the right hands it could do a lot of good for the universe. The trouble is there aren't many good hands about.'

'That depends on what you define as good.'

'True,' he agreed. 'But I doubt that you'll qualify.'

'I...Amun-Ra, the Emperor of the Osirans, defy qualification. It is my destiny.'

'No, you see you are wrong. No-one has a god given right to this thing, not even a god such as yourself. It should not belong to any one person, especially one who thinks they deserve it.'

'Who are you to judge?'

'I'm not, but I'll tell you what I am. I'm the person who currently has it.'

'Not for long.'

'What are you going to do? Take it from me?'

'But of course. But before we do, we have a little gift for the peoples of this repulsive world.'

'That's a bit harsh calling this world repulsive, I mean look at it. I think it's rather beautiful.'

'That depends on what you define as beautiful...' said Amun-Ra. 'In beauty I see fire. The universe awash with flames, I see a new order. I see the...Flux...in my hands and I see the Osirans as untouchable gods!'

'Sounds more like a nightmare to me,' said Random.

'It matters not, you will be living in it soon.'

A massive hole began to open in the underside of the pyramid.

'What's that?' asked Random.

'Your end,' Amun-Ra roared.

Random started to panic. He held the Flux above his head.

'You even think about blowing these people away and I'll use it.'

Amun-Ra stalled.

'You wouldn't dare...'

'Wouldn't I? I suppose that's what you've got to consider...'

'One swift twist of this cell and the Flux can be unleashed. I will be able to bend it to my will. It will be able to destroy you. So why run that risk, eh? Why not go now and never come back?'

'Are you trying to bargain with me, puny insect?' Amun-Ra was impressed. 'You are indeed a brave one.'

Random winced. 'Why not go home, use this immense power to put a stop to the war?'

He grew very concerned.

The voices were back.

'Think of how you could use the Flux, Random, to bring peace to Rodas. Put an end to all the hurt...the suffering?'

The voices were overwhelming.

Over and over again these two sentences bounded around inside his skull.

'Please...' he said, redirecting his efforts back to the Osiran fleet. 'Do the sensible thing and leave.'

'In no time at all this world will be nothing. Pulped. Pulverised. Squashed like an ant hill under a heavy boot. You with it. Your life is of no consequence to us. In fact, we would take much joy in destroying you and the rest of the pitiful inhabitants of this world.'

'But these people have no other home, you'd be committing genocide!' cried our Random. He looked at the Flux. It began to call to him…

*

Anji, Jake and the others were trying to work out what Random was saying, but being such a distance away, it was to no avail. Strakonis had the advantage of being that much closer and he was starting to worry about Random's position. As he finished tending to his wounds he placed a concerned hand on his forehead.

'Don't do it, Random. For all that's good in the universe, don't!'

*

'These people are nothing! You don't know them. Why are you willing to risk your life to save their worthless existence?' asked Amun-Ra.

'Because their existence is not worthless!' said Random. His hand clasped the release mechanism on the cell.

Amun-Ra grew concerned. 'I am going to give you five seconds to power down your weapons or so help me…'

Random pleaded with his conscience. If he used the Flux, he would be saving the millions, nay billions of inhabitants on Spectronia, but he'd be committing mass murder, no, genocide himself if he just twisted the cell. Could he really do that? Destroy an entire civilisation if it meant the salvation of another. Maybe it was his calling to be judge, jury and executioner. After all, he was destined to put an end to war on Rodas. Why couldn't he end it anywhere else?

'Prepare to fire the Armageddon beam!' Amun-Ra barked to his fellow gods.

The hum of the beam grew stronger. The link was complete.

Shivering, sweating, Random looked down over the canyon ridge and saw swathes of people. Spectronians, looking up at him. Counting on him.

Then he saw Anji and Jake and his faithful Skateboard. How could he let them perish? He'd never allow anything to happen to them or the Spectronians.

No. He had to do it. He would have to live with his decision.

As the voices in his mind reached a crescendo, Random looked up at the pyramid.

'You asked for it.'

'Fire now!' cried Amun-Ra.

Random opened the cell and the Flux exploded in his hands. The purple boy was swathed in green energy. He cried out in pain and horror as the Flux seeped through every pore in his being, consuming him completely. As he continued to be overwhelmed by its power, he began to levitate high into the air.

*

Anji and Jake were horrified, their faces awash with alarm and Skateboard, who had turned up his audio bandwidth and listened to the whole exchange without telling the others, was shocked by the events unfolding in front of him.

Meanwhile in his ship, Strakonis fell to the floor in shock.

He had told Random not to open the Flux.

Random hadn't listened.

Now all manner of hell was about to be unleashed on Spectronia.

XXVI

Random let the Flux explore every cell of his body.
He felt it surge like a monsoon throughout him, but
at no point was he afraid, nor was he out of control.
He let the Flux work him out, just as much as it let
him look into what made it so powerful. Random
couldn't find any malice within it. He also could
not see any reason to be as consumed with greed
for the power that it could bring him like it had
Lon.

The Flux could sense no reason to distrust him
either. His intentions were true. If he wanted, he
could be the true owner of it but Random had no
need for it, he felt, and still felt.

The Flux was safe.

But it sensed the conflict in Random's mind.
There was something going on in there it did not
understand. Was it enough for it to reject him as a
host?

Random concentrated hard to block the same two
voices that had plagued him since his birth out. He
needed all of his will power to obliterate the
Osirans. He was beyond doubt. He was ready.

Random's eyes glowed emerald green. He
readied his hands towards the pyramid fleet. Like
bolts of lightning, the Flux exploded towards
Amun-Ra's pyramid.

The god stood his ground. Accepting his fate, he thrust his arms wide open and allowed the wave of armageddon to blow him away.

Molecule by molecule, the pyramids were hit by the green wave that irradiated from Random's fingers, rocking in the sky like ships in a storm.

*

Anji, Jake, Skateboard, Solenia and the surviving Spectronians watch aghast as they witnessed the green wave wash over the Osiran's ships and bit by bit, they began to melt away to nothingness. Moment by moment the pyramids were fading into nothingness. Before long, all of them had disappeared and the green wave swept back into Random's body.

The Osirans had been obliterated.

Random exhaled deeply. The Flux flowed out of his mouth, sweeping back towards its cell and within moments, Random had his feet firmly back on the ground and the Flux was safely back in his housing.

He looked down gratefully at his friends far below and watched as Anji and Jake got on Skateboard's back and they made towards him.

Random smiled as he saw the Spectronians cheering and heard them whooping and celebrating the end of terror.

The threat was over. Random had saved the day.

However as Solenia and Strakonis looked up at him from their vantage points, they were far from happy…

Random had done it.

Saved yet another civilisation from a doom that this time he had inadvertently brought upon them himself.

He would have to take responsibility for those who had perished, but as with his decision to wipe the Osirans out, he would have to learn to live with that burden.

Burden.

That was a word he was becoming used to.

He stood up and drank in the sound of silence.

Then his eyes grew wide with happiness.

Silence.

The voices had stopped.

They were gone!

He gave out a little chuckle to himself and went to pick the Flux, which was trapped in its holding cell again, calm as a white cloud in a sunny sky, but his vision suddenly went a little out of focus.

As he heard Anji calling out his name, he suddenly felt his body grow very weary. He slumped onto the floor and stayed there until his friends joined him.

'Random mate, that was awesome!' said Jake, thumping his friend's upper arm as he sat cross legged next to him.

'Random, you did it! But what happened to them?' asked Anji.

Random gave a weary look. The colour was drained from his face. He looked gaunt, unwell, older than his age. 'The Osirans…no more…had to…'

'Random? Anji took his hand. He was really hot to touch.

Before Anji could get an answer, Random had slumped into Jake's lap, leading the blonde haired boy to feel quite uncomfortable.

'Uh…Anj?'

Skateboard ran a medical scan on Random.

'He appears to be asleep. The Flux must have drained all of his energy from him. If you could put him on my back I would greatly oblige.'

Solenia and Strakonis had taken one of the rainbow roads up to the vantage point and made it just as the two human teenagers were bundling Random onto their robot friend.

'How is he?' asked Solenia.

'Stable but unconscious,' replied Skateboard. 'He will be fine in no time.'

'And the Flux?' she enquired.

Strakonis let out a wheezing groan as he got down to pick the Flux's cell up off the dirt.

'Intact and neutralised.'

'Good,' she said before turning her attention to the travellers. 'What your friend did we shall be forever grateful for. But I cannot ignore that he committed genocide here on my world.'

'He saved your people, didn't he?' said Anji defiantly.

'Take a look down there,' Solenia ordered.

Anji and Jake peered over the precipice and saw many Spectronians celebrating their salvation, but it was hard to ignore the dead bodies that littered the canyon like a battlefield fresh from war.

'Many of my people will never see another sunrise. They paid the price for the danger that you all brought to Spectronia.'

'Your Majesty-' Skateboard butted in.

'Silence!' she barked.

The trio uttered not a word.

'We Spectronians pride ourselves on peace and non-interference. You have brought death to our door. Despite your good deeds, I hereby banish you all from Spectronia forthwith.'

'But he saved your lives!' shouted Anji.

'You can tell him how thankful we all are when he comes around but not here. Go to your ship, leave and never come back!'

Anji and Jake were stunned and ashamed.

'We shall do as you please, your Majesty,' said Skateboard. 'We can do nothing more than follow your orders and apologise for the harm we have brought you.'

Solenia stared them down.

'Come on, you two,' said Skateboard sadly. 'Back to the Venus II.'

'Can't we say goodbye?' asked Jake.

'No.' said Skateboard firmly.

With their heads bowed like scolded children, Anji and Jake followed Skateboard back onto the rainbow road and slowly they disappeared from sight.

'Your Majesty,' said Strakonis, 'Not that it is for me to argue with your excellency but was that a little harsh?'

'You know the power of the Flux,' she replied. 'You saw it with your own eyes as well as I saw with mine. Thanks to their intervention a whole race has just been obliterated in the skies of my world. Their blood is now a stain on our history. For centuries to come my people will talk about the day that gods fell to the might of one man, consumed by the most brilliant power in the entire galaxy. And you expect me to hide it here?'

Strakonis bowed his head. She had a point. He had warned Random not to use it. Indeed, he was surprised at how well he had contained it inside him.

'But his actions led to the survival of your race. Without him you would all be extinct.'

'This is true, which is why I have let them go freely. You do understand that we cannot be the keepers of the Flux now, don't you Strakonis?'

The explorer nodded sadly. 'Yes, I understand.'

'Will you be able to find somewhere else to hide it as quickly as you can?'

'I will, someday.' He patted the cell and the Flux gave out a little hum. 'Although no one is looking for it now, it will still be hunted, I'm sure.'

'Then I wish you luck in your quest,' Solenia did not wait for a response and made her way back to her Doa, who with a click of her heels reared up and turned away.

'Farewell Strakonis and good luck.'

Strakonis held up his hand as Solenia rode away and left him alone with the Flux.

Unabated this time with no-one chasing him, it was up to him to leave the Flux on a remote, technologically stilted planet where no one would think of looking.

He walked back to his ship, deep in thought. What was the name of that planet he had thought of before Spectronia but decided against due to lack of fuel reserves on his ship?

What was it called? That one in the solar system with the primitive people who hadn't even got any further than their own moon when it came to space travel?

Strakonis wracked his brains and decided that as soon as his engines were back up and running, and that he had remembered the name of this elusive world, that he would set a course and hide the Flux there, somewhere.

Surely the people of that world wouldn't be as dangerous as his now dead rival, Lon…

XXVII

It had taken the travellers a few hours to get back
to the Venus II and on their long trek home they
had barely said a word to one another.

It was weird to them not having Random to keep
them company on their return to the Venus II and
although he was there in body, he wasn't there in
spirit. He was sleeping like a baby, flat out on his
front. Anji had manufactured a blanket out of his
combat jacket, covering his torso so she could see
nothing else other than a ball of hair protruding
from underneath it.

She felt hot. Whether she was warm from the sun
or from the shame of being banished, she couldn't
tell.

A part of her had sympathised with Solenia. She
was Queen. She had to protect her people and
sadly, some of them had lost their lives. But that
hadn't been Random's fault. The Osirans would
have caught up with them eventually, if they had
crash landed on Spectronia or not. It was just
unfortunate but she didn't feel bad that Random
had gone to the extremes that he had. He'd saved a
peaceful race, wiped out an evil too. Surely what
he did wasn't all that bad?

She looked at his unmoving frame again, still
except for signs of normal breathing as the coat
rose and fell with every snore.

'There she is!' Jake said gleefully.

The Venus II stood proudly before them.

When the gleaming seda metal and shiny hull of their vessel honed into view, all three of them had felt such a relief.

'It looks as good as new!' exclaimed Jake.

'So it should be, given the calculations in the self-repair unit,' said Skateboard, who had connected back remotely with the ship as he was now in distance and had already turned the oxygen, gravity and landing lights on. With a hiss of hydraulics, the ramp that led up to the mid-section hissed as it landed softly in the colourful sand.

'It feels like ages since we've been away from you old thing, we've missed you!' said Anji.

'It can't hear you,' Jake tutted.

'I'll pass your kind words on, miss,' said Skateboard.

They all made their way up the ramp and were pleasantly shocked to see the interior was in such good condition too. For a ship that was ripped apart, gutted even in its recent crash landing, the living area looked like someone had given it a spring clean!

'Amazing!' said Anji.

'We'd better wake up Random,' said Jake. 'I'd have thought he'd have been awake by now.'

'To be fair to him he did absorb the most powerful thing in the universe,' said Anji.

'I'm sure that all he needs is to recharge his batteries, something I am never forgetting to do again,' joked Skateboard. 'Now, do me a favour will you please? Take him to his quarters so I can get us up in the air will you?'

'Sure, anything to get away from this colourful mess of a planet!' said Jake.

'That's a bit rude, man,' said Anji.

'Well, they didn't even thank us did they? And I never got to say goodbye to Row.'

'Whose Row?'

Jake went hot with embarrassment.

'Uh, no-one!'

Anji knelt down to pick Random up, who had been face down on Skateboard's back for the best part of a few hours now. She went to pick him up by his arm and then noticed something that was not right.

'Hold on.'

Jake's attention was diverted from daydreaming about the crush he was never going to see again down to the call of his friend.

'Jake! Anji sounded panicked.

She rolled Random over.

The two of them recoiled in horror.

'Skateboard, what's happened to Random?'

Anji and Jake stood back, unable to process what had happened to their alien friend.

Gone was Random's unique purple complexion.

He had changed colour.

He was red and blue, split down the middle.
One half crimson.
The other half a sapphire blue!

ACKNOWLEDGEMENTS

The author would like to thank the following people for their contribution, support, words of encouragement and general awesomeness. My wife, Sophie, Anthony Moorin for yet another brilliant set of artwork, Nicola Currie, Tom Savill-Owen, Anna Brown, Stephen D'Costa, the Diddly Dummers, Mark Cockram, Iain Martin, Simon Brett and VC Covers.

Most of all, to anyone who has picked up this book and enjoyed it. It really means so much!

The adventures of Captain Random will continue
in *The Stratos Conundrum*.

Also Available:

The Lurking

ISBN: 978-1999865955

Rob is a hopeless loser in the game of life. With work, his relationship with his long suffering girlfriend Claire, with everything in general. Tonight he will change for the better, make a fresh start by taking it to the next step and propose to her.

But fate has other intentions.

After an accident that leaves him stranded, Rob takes shelter in an abandoned aircraft hangar and soon discovers that he is not alone. There is something lurking in the darkness, taunting him, haunting his every movement.

Soon trapped in a living nightmare, Rob must learn the terrible truth of his tormentor and escape its clutches before it is too late...

Available from all good book shops.

Captain Random and the Eater of Souls

ISBN: 978-1999865931

Following their explosive battle with the Sandman, and struggling to come to terms with life out in space, the crew of the Venus II decide to throw themselves into a spot of retail therapy on the friendly planet of Genocia.

But almost as soon as they arrive, they realise that this new world is not all that it seems. Outside the splendour and vast wealth of the Grand Chamber lies a neglected wasteland where terror lurks within the poisonous gloom whilst deep within the bowels of the planet lies a terrible secret.

At the very heart of it all is the ruthless leader Consula, whose designs for supremacy mean ultimate devastation to all of those who oppose her. But the greed and corruption of the government is nothing compared to what lurks in the shadows for Random and his friends. Separated and fighting for their lives, Random, Anji, Jake and Skateboard must work quickly to save the lives of the prisoners stuck in the mines deep below the surface, where death is very close by...

What is the Soul Destroyer? What part does it play in Consula's diabolical plan? Will Anji ever see her friends again? One thing is for sure. The Eater of Souls is hungry...

Available from all good book shops.

Captain Random vs the Sandman

ISBN: 978-1999865924

Rodas. The scorned planet of Ursa-17. Ravaged by centuries of war between two factions, the villainous Sapphire Regime and the ruthless Crimson Empire. The reason behind the conflict of red and blue? The people of Rodas were unable to make the colour purple.
Until one day, when two rebels, one from either side, combine to create the ultimate warrior. A being who could put an end to the battle of ages and bring peace to the volatile planet of Rodas once and for all.

There is one tiny drawback. The warrior is a boy.

***** Fantastic book, enjoyed every part of it!
Highly recommend it for Dr Who/Red Dwarf/Rick and Morty fans.

***** Hayden Gribble's writing is witty and clever with an essence of Douglas Adams in there too.Would thoroughly recommend for anyone with an adventurous spirit.

***** I really enjoyed it. I can well imagine Kids getting swept along with the interstellar, action packed adventure and chuckling along with all the funny scenarios and characters and wanting to know just what happens .

Available from all good book shops.

Child Out of Time: Growing Up With Doctor Who in the Wilderness Years

ISBN: 978-1999865900

For 26 years, DOCTOR WHO was a British institution, capturing the imaginations of generations of children. But then, in 1989, it was cancelled. The Doctor and his on-screen adventures were no more. There was no longer a hero, a champion for the outcasts who struggled to fit in. It was as though he had walked into his TARDIS and set his controls for dematerialisation, never to return: a whole generation lost to the powers of Science Fiction's greatest creation. It was in this Doctor-less world that I grew up. This is the story of how one little boy would try to find the Doctor in any way, shape or form and the obstacles he faced in doing so. This is the story of growing up without Doctor Who in the Wilderness Years…and how I lived through it.

***** An engaging and enjoyable insight into a fan discovering Doctor Who during the wilderness years

***** A very passionate account of one fans discovery of the greatest science fiction of all time.

**** Perfect for fans of the Doctor in any of his or her forms.

Available from all good book shops.

The Man In The Corner

ISBN: 978-1500549862

A mysterious assassin wants out of his life as a cold and ruthless killer but must face one last assignment before he flicks the escape switch. As he closes in on the biggest criminal mind in the country, he is reminded of what he left behind and how getting closer to the light at the end of the tunnel might also reunite him with a person from his long and distant past. Who is the Big Chief? Why must he be brought down and will it be the end, not just for himself and his superior, but also to the only link to the life he has lost.

***** An exciting book! Whilst focusing on the dark story of an unnamed man, you find yourself sucked into a city of criminals. The chapters contain their own stories which really draw you in and make you want to read more. Great read! The only negative is that it was over too fast.

***** Brilliant read. Did not want to put the book down.

*** This book is a great little read about the path to redemption; not too long, in fact in some places I found myself wishing it might go on a little longer. It's got a sort of style all its own.

Available from all good book shops.

Hayden Gribble was born in Cambridge in June 1989. He has always loved writing and released his debut novel, The Man In The Corner, as an ebook in 2013 before it went paperback the following year.

Captain Random and the Rainbow Chasers is his seventh book and the third in the Captain Random saga.

Away from writing, Hayden loves reading, walking, sports, music, film and TV.

He has also been a regular member of the Diddly Dum Podcast, a show about Doctor Who, since February 2015 and curates his own James Bond podcast, Podcasters Royale. Both can be found on iTunes.

He lives with his family in Suffolk.

www.ingramcontent.com/pod-product-compliance
Lightning Source LLC
Chambersburg PA
CBHW072030220726

48293CB00016B/611